Second Go-Round

Elite Escorts 3

Lynn Burke

Second Go-Round

Christine watched her father grieve over losing his soul mate.

I survived the devastating effects of my parent's ugly divorce due to my childhood leukemia.

Now, both our jaded hearts are closed off to anything outside hookups.

But my emotions get tangled up in our first attempt at sating each other's lust, and I yearn for more than spending my nights as an escort.

I want a second go-round with Christine.

While her walls appear invincible, an act of terror in our city tumbles them down leaving her bruised and broken with no hope of escape.

Will I be strong enough to see her through the darkest time of her life? Or will the rubble of destruction keep me from finding love with the woman I long for?

Chapter 1

Christine

Nothing like Saturday mornings, a pot of coffee, and sports radio on TV. While Nick and Nate chatted about the upcoming football season onscreen, I sucked down caffeine, hoping it would infuse my bloodstream with wakefulness so I wouldn't have to prop my eyelids open with toothpicks to make it through the day.

A guy had kept me up too late but not because of mind-blowing orgasms. Talk about a lousy lay.

I swallowed down more coffee and shook my head, my mind flitting to memories of my dating app dude from the night before. The sexually charged energy over the dinner table. The grinding of his huge hard-on against my ass while we had danced amidst strobe lights and thumping bass. The anticipation heating my blood as I'd dragged him into my house at one in the morning.

We hadn't made it into the bedroom, ending up going at it right there on my couch because I'd been too damn hungry for cock to even think about christening my new king-sized bed.

Unfortunately, the guy didn't know how to use the package he'd been blessed with. That and his complete lack of hand and mouth use on my body killed it for me. And not in a good way. He had just stuck his dick in and went to town, getting his own rocks off and leaving me scrambling to keep up. The entire affair had been passionless and forgettable.

Boring with a capital B.

Stifling a yawn, I frowned and shuffled into my living room. I shouldn't have been surprised by my night's end. Every man I'd been out with since losing my virginity back in high school had pretty much proven to be the same. Energy, hype, then disappointment because men need a clit road map. I climaxed most of the time, but only because I had to help them get the job done.

You'd have thought I had ripped the guy's heart out when I showed him the door after finishing—and declining his suggestion of going on a second date.

Broken heart number fifty? Sixty? Whatever the number, he joined all the men I'd left hanging or begging for another chance at rocking my world. The very few who happened to talk me into one more tumble between the sheets ended up as a similar blip on the radar of my past, blocked and ignored.

I'd been called all kinds of nasty names over the years for my playgirl ways, but they weren't wrong in their conclusions of my being a cold-hearted bitch who just wanted sex. I liked men. I loved to fuck. But my heart wasn't available, and one-night stands ensured no feels got involved.

Having witnessed my father lose the love of his life and seeing the emotional hardship he endured for all those years since Mom had passed made me wary of commitment.

While he claimed it was better to have loved Mom and lost her than to never have known her love, I disagreed. I couldn't imagine a soulmate being ripped away with such violence. She'd been my mother, and that had been hard enough of a loss to endure.

Countless hours of therapy with and without Dad had taught me how to deal with the sorrow, but it lingered. Always would—same as my nightmares of engulfing flames. Smoke. Screams I'd never actually heard outside my dreams.

But watching Dad break down had been the deciding factor that had shaped my life when it came to relationships. No way in hell would I allow a man to burrow his way into my soul and stake a claim on my heart like my mom had done with my dad then leave me devastated at their loss.

Huffing an exhale over my latest failed attempt at earth-shattering sex, I sprawled on the couch and turned my focus on the TV. Nick informed those listening in that the Patriot's rookie tight end, Jackson, had messed up his knee at practice the day before. They weren't sure he'd be on the field the next afternoon to help kick off the season.

Jackson had been a first-round draft pick, and I'd had high hopes since Dad and I would be sitting in the stands as always, getting to watch him rule the field.

"Shit," I muttered at the same time my cell dinged.

I fished my phone from my robe pocket and flipped it over. Dad knew better than to contact me before nine on a Saturday morning, but this update from our favorite sports radio talk show host would have him chatting up a storm. I swiped my thumb over the screen and sipped.

Dad: **Have you seen the news?**

I used one hand to reply, **Just now. Think he'll be**

able to play?

Dad: **Huh?**

Me: **Our rookie with the injury. Aren't you listening to Nick and Nate?**

Dad: **Shit. No, I haven't heard about that. I'm talking about the latest bomb threat.**

"Fuck." I set aside my mug. He wouldn't be texting me unless a business our family insured was involved.

I quickly texted Dad back that I hadn't, dropped my cell, and clicked the TV channel over to NECN.

There had been a few bomb threats to some of Boston's downtown queer-owned businesses in the previous weeks, one of which had led to an explosion. Although no individual—or group—had claimed responsibility for the tragic loss of sixteen lives, I expected it was probably some religious fanatics believing they needed to cleanse the world of so-called sin.

The latest had threatened the Blushing Cherry, one of our long-standing customers at Gemberling Insurance. No evidence of a bomb had been found according to the news anchor and everyone had been evacuated safely, but still. I'd bet the owner lost a shit ton of money that night because of it. I also wondered how many faithful patrons would stay holed up at home in the coming weeks.

"Damnit." I put my empty mug on the coffee table and texted a mad face back to my dad.

The police needed to catch the bastards robbing Boston's nightlife businesses and traumatizing their LGBTQ+ owners. While the bomb hadn't kept me from visiting my favorite dance clubs and bars downtown, the crowds had certainly lessened since the threats had begun earlier in the summer.

My phone rang as images of the BC showed on-screen behind the newswoman, a bar/strip joint I was well acquainted with. While I didn't get turned on by watching other women rip off their clothes, I loved the sexually charged energy pulsing through the air. All that testosterone building...needing release.

I swiped to answer, setting aside thoughts of the unsatisfying dick the night before. "Hey, Jessie."

"Did you see the news?" my good friend and employee asked without a preamble.

A click on the remote muted the TV. "I just turned it on after Dad texted me about it."

"Isn't that David's place?"

A huffed, annoyed exhale caused me to sag back into the couch again, and I retrieved my coffee, thinking about how David and his partner Lawrence had to be feeling that morning. "Yep."

"Cassie!" Jessie's muffled holler at her young daughter sounded loud over the line. "I told you not to touch!"

Cassie yelled something unintelligible in the background while Jessie fumbled with her cell, filling my ear with thumps and clatters.

"Sorry," she said a few seconds later. "Cassie's new obsession with the Keurig is driving me nuts."

I eyed the last inch of coffee in my mug and went into the kitchen to pour another. "She's got good taste." Meandering around the island, I made for the coffeepot. "How is little Bossy-Boo?"

"Bossy as ever." Jess huffed. "And haven't nearly hit the worst years yet. I will either enter a mental hospital or turn into a wino when this kid becomes a teenager."

A soft chuckle escaped me as I refilled my cup. At least Jessie would have Reid by her side to help her out when the time came. Dad and I had placed bets on their engagement. He'd said by Christmas, but I expected Reid wouldn't wait that long.

I had introduced the two of them earlier in the spring—or rather, Reid had been an escort at the time, and I'd hired him to show my single mom friend a fun night on the town. I'd gone to school with Reid, and he'd always been a forever kind of guy. He'd fallen hard for Jessie after one date, and it had taken a while, but Jessie finally caved to being his. I expected they would live happily ever after.

I hoped for the best for both of them even though I'd sworn off love, heart eyes, and declarations of futures with white picket fences.

"How was your hookup last night?" Jessie whispered as though attempting to hide her words from Cassie.

"Same old, same old," I muttered while leaning my hip against the kitchen counter and lifting my mug.

"That bad, huh?"

"Worst lay of my life." I sipped, sighing inwardly over the black, bitter brew warming my throat. "He had the perfect tool shed and equipment, but that man could make water dry with his lack of knowledge on how to use them."

"Ugh."

"Yeah, but it's probably a good thing he didn't. You know how much I want to get my heart invested."

Jessie sighed. I hadn't told her the full story of how my dad had lost my mom. Discussing that kind of grief hurt too much to relive. "Sounds like you need something to perk you up."

"If the coffee isn't doing it, nothing will," I said, keeping our conversation light.

"Hmm. Actually, I think I have just the thing."

"Doubt it." I sipped again, contemplating a low-carb

breakfast when all I wanted was bacon and thick slabs of French toast doused in maple syrup. A side of home fries would taste damn good too.

"Reid finally fulfilled his end of the bargain."

Food ideas flitting to the back of my mind, I perked up all right—wide fucking awake.

I had let Reid bribe me a couple of months earlier into giving him Jessie's phone number. In exchange, he'd agreed to land me a free night with one of his ex-co-workers from Elite Escorts. Tall, dark, and handsome, pretty boy Jarod. At least, that was what his profile on Elite's website portrayed him to be.

"Seriously?" I heard myself squeak while telling myself the guy probably just photographed well.

"Yep. There was a last-minute cancellation for tonight, so Reid got your file bumped up in line."

"Holy shit. Oh, holy *fucking* shit." Gone were the thoughts of a lousy lay and the exhaustion tugging on my eyelids. Energy sparkled inside of me, priming me to life in both my mind and core.

Jessie laughed. "I gave Reid your email address for Elite to send over the forms. Personal info, limits...all that good stuff."

I bit on my thumbnail, eyeing the pile of dishes in the sink.

Limits.

I wouldn't even know what they were. I had fantasies out the yin-yang but had yet to meet a sampling from the smorgasbord of man-beef who was interested in learning what desires crowded my mind.

Exhibitionism. Rough sex that included just enough pain to arouse. Maybe a little chokehold. Tease the shit out of me, deny me a climax, make me beg for it...but some of the things I fantasized about weren't exactly hookup safe. They needed to be in a relationship with a man I could trust.

I snorted. "Not happening."

Or with a hired professional...

I'd never checked out any of the BDSM joints downtown even though I'd heard a rumor there was one owned by a woman named Chantelle that operated as an invite-only club. But I didn't know anyone in the lifestyle, and I wasn't sure that was exactly what I had in mind.

Was there such a thing as soft BDSM?

A few minutes later, I hung up the phone and eyed the sink full of dishes. I expected my entire house would be spotless before noon as I tried to make the time pass. The hours would probably stretch on for an eternity while my mind went overboard imagining the night ahead of me.

Elite Escort Jarod.

The memory of his full-length pic on the website flitted through my brain. Luscious-lipped, muscles rippling over his bare chest and down his torso...and I couldn't forget the bulge in his boxer briefs.

My mouth watered, and I bit back a groan, closing my eyes briefly.

"God, I hope you're all that and more," I whispered to the image in my head.

The problem was, if Jarod lived up to my expectations, the available males I tended to land for a night of fun would fall *way* short of satisfying me rather than just the mediocre I'd been accepting.

Sighing, I pulled on rubber gloves and went to town, ready for the hours to pass as fast as possible.

I had a date with a hunk of burning sex on legs—and I kept my fingers crossed he would deliver.

Chapter 2

Jarod

I stared at the file emailed over from Dina at Elite Escorts.

Christine Gemberling was a friend of Reid and his girlfriend, Jessica. I'd been informed by Reid what he'd done to get Jessica's number—and warned that Christine was my type. He had also suggested I would need to guard my heart.

But I didn't have much of a heart to bother with. What remained of the vulnerable side of me had gotten locked up years earlier and would never see the light of day again. I always took care to make sure no one would threaten the safe environment I'd created for myself by controlling who had access to my inner sanctuary.

That included studying the profiles Dina sent me to better plan out the evening ahead. While I considered my night job an outlet for my wild side, I never entered into a situation unarmed emotionally.

The last-minute client assigned to me included a professional headshot of a green-eyed beauty with fiery red hair falling in waves over her shoulders. Her smile suggested playful. Perhaps untamed as a feral kitty. Definitely a flirt.

My cock began to swell at thoughts of watching her full lips clamping around my length and sucking me deep.

She's fucking fine.

I cleared my throat and adjusted myself inside of my scrubs beneath the break room table. Ignoring the steak-tip salad I'd brought along for lunch in front of me, I flipped back to the specs for that night's one-on-one date.

Twenty-nine, I noted, from the North Shore area, loves beer, football, and sex.

"Huh." Brow furrowed, I reread that line. She was definitely my kind of woman if I had been looking for one.

As with every Elite customer I'd been booked with, I went through her paperwork, noting and memorizing what she did and didn't want. What got her off. What turned her on. I enjoyed everything about women's bodies and satisfying them, but I loved being in control of the situation just as much. The better to protect myself from heartache.

I didn't do impulsive, so having ready pussy at my fingertips by way of a nighttime job of being an escort fit my life perfectly. It was my outlet, the only sexual freedom I allowed myself.

One last eyeful of Christine's pic and I clicked out of the file and rang Reid's number.

"Zimmerman. What's up?" he answered after a couple of rings.

"Hey, Sullivan. Just got a file from Dina."

He chuckled. "She's Jessie's boss, the one who I had to bribe into giving me her number."

"Yeah, I remember you telling me about her."

Christine had originally booked a date with me for her friend back in April, but I had gotten sick earlier in the day from some bad Thai food. Reid had filled in for me. Tall, dark, and handsome, both of our Elite profiles promised, exactly what Christine had been looking for to gift her friend a night on the town without responsibilities.

"From what I've heard," Reid said, "she's a wildcat in the sack, so you'll definitely have a good time."

"Oh, I plan on it." I always did.

"And I know you claim you don't have a heart to lose—"

"Don't worry," I cut him off, knowing exactly what he was going to reiterate. "I can keep things professional." No woman had ever tempted me to cross an emotional line. Having witnessed the lack of loyalty between my parents when I'd been a kid, I wouldn't allow myself the weakness of putting my heart in someone else's hands.

"Good. So how's work going?"

Glancing around the empty break room, I grinned, fully content in my life. "Nursing or fucking?"

Sullivan laughed. "The fucking-for-the-money night job."

"Still pays better than my daytime position," I answered with a wry grin. "Not quite as fun without you though, man."

"Yeah, those were the days." Reid huffed another laugh. "No more threesomes for me."

"Yeah, yeah." I stabbed one of the steak tips with my plastic fork. "You've been skipping out when the guys' get-togethers too. I've pretty much given up on the old crew. Micah, his brother, and the new hire, Cooney, are coming over for the game tomorrow. You gonna be around?"

"Jessie and I have plans."

I rolled my eyes. Of course, he did—the same as my other friends that had been disappearing left and right due to offering their necks for a ball and chain.

"Keep in touch, will you?" I tossed out, not exactly exuberant about how lives changed around me.

"Sure thing, Zimmerman. Take it easy—but not on Christine. Jessica says she's a kinky one who'll give any man who knows what he's doing a run for his money."

We would see about that.

I hung up a minute later, shoveled the steak into my mouth, and reopened the image of Christine.

She wanted to meet at a dance place downtown. Thumping music, strobe lights, and those lips. I adjusted myself again. I sure as hell hoped she had some flesh to hold onto. With a face like that, a cushioned body for fucking, a beer *and* Patriots lover?

I just might fall in love.

With a derisive snort, I exited out of the file and put my phone down. Thanks to my parents' shit marriage and ugly divorce after I'd gone into remission as a kid, I had sworn off relationships.

I chewed a piece of stringy steak, my brow furrowed. Soulmates didn't exist. That's why I enjoyed my night job with Elite. Get paid for sex, no attachments. Ever.

Sure, a handful of women had claimed to love me as they'd come around my cock, but who didn't have that second or two of emotion when finding release? Who didn't want to stay in that suspended-in-time high of euphoria and adrenaline forever?

Another peek at those green eyes and lush lips...*Christine.*

Fuck me. I couldn't wait.

"Jarod?"

I turned at Doctor Carr's voice. The woman was sexy as hell with curves in all the right places but definitely a high-maintenance princess who didn't have a damn thing in common with me outside of wanting to care for sick children.

Also, I didn't fuck around with fellow employees.

"What's up, Wendy?" I asked the petite brunette behind me.

"Mary Rose needs a visit from her favorite nurse."

Shit. I quickly shoved my lunch stuff away even though I had a good ten minutes of break left. The little girl Wendy spoke of was new to the hospital. She'd been diagnosed with terminal leukemia, and one look at the smiling cherub had ripped my heart out.

Attending to sick kids had become my childhood goal after experiencing some of the best care with my own nurses. While my parents had been busy throwing accusations and blame for my illness at each other, the hospital's kind caretakers had given me words of affirmation and edification. Theirs had been the gentle hands helping me when I'd been too sick to function without help and Mom had been too occupied with licking her own emotional wounds to give me what I needed.

It had been a blessing my parents had split. Being tossed from one house to the other after beating cancer's ass hadn't been pleasant, but at least I didn't have to deal with the toxicity of them being up in each other's space.

Her grandparents raised Mary Rose. I hadn't gotten the scoop on where her parents were, but it didn't matter when her grandpop and grandmama lavished attention on her hurting body and sweet spirit. The young girl faced death without hope of remission, but she would feel loved until her final breath.

Chest aching, I thanked Wendy for letting me know I'd been summoned by my favorite little patient.

Mary Rose's dark curls were long gone due to treatment, and although her cancer spread too rapidly to control, she still faced every moment with a smile and positivity.

It was my job—my passion and reason for having survived cancer—to make sure she had the support to keep that outlook to the end.

Thoughts of Elite and the redheaded beauty I'd have beneath me that night took a backseat to what I loved the most about my life.

Putting a smile on my face, I knocked and entered Mary Rose's room to see how I could be of service.

Chapter 3

Christine

Most of the time, karma was a bitch.

Lucky me, she'd come back to *kiss* my ass rather than kick it like usual.

Elite Escorts didn't come cheap, and the only reason I'd been able to afford to set Jessie up with one had been because my dad had given me a bonus for all my hard work at our family business the prior quarter. Sure, I'd tucked some extra pennies away for myself and that overseas trip I'd been planning for years, but my friend had been floundering.

And I'd sacrificed a bit of my own extra to gift her something she'd desperately needed.

I'd even chosen the escort I would have gotten for myself if I'd been willing to hire a dick for a hot date.

Jarod Zimmerman.

Reid had ended up replacing him that night and taking Jessica out, so things had turned out as they were meant to... and karma decided to be kind to me for my giving spirit. At least, I saw shit that way.

But I'd always been like my mom in that I gave until it

hurt, both with my time and empathy. Too often, people took advantage of my goodness, but life was short, and we had to live our potential to the fullest. Enjoy every second. Soak up every chance to experience new, exciting things.

All it took was one moment, one breath, one second for tragedy to strike.

I'd done a lot of shit in my twenty-nine years, but a night on the town with a paid escort who was sure to please and satisfy my sexual hunger had to be the most luscious opportunity to arise.

Since I didn't want to waste one minute wining and dining at some upscale restaurant like I'd bought for Jessie with her escort, I requested Jarod meet me at my favorite dance club downtown. We could get straight to the grinding, the touching, the heightening of arousal for...after.

Goose bumps pebbled over my entire body at the fantasy of having Jarod's hands on my body. He would know where to touch me. His experienced tongue would travel over me without hesitation, locating my yummy spots and pleasure places in order to send me soaring.

Talk about high expectations.

I had them—with a capital E.

Antsy and impatient as always, I found myself ready to roll an hour early. Freshly showered and shaved, dressed to fucking *kill* in my short skirt and plunging neckline blouse that barely contained the girls, I decided to just head out and grab a drink and get my groove on before Jarod even arrived.

My cell rang, stalling me from walking out the door.

"Hey, Dad." I always answered if and when he rang. Allowing a loved one's phone call to go to voicemail had been his biggest regret. We'd learned our lesson the hardest way imaginable.

At least we still had Mom's recording, her final words to both of us from when we had been too busy at Fenway watching the Sox play to answer. Had we known the house burned down around her, that afternoon would have gone differently. Still tragic with all hope of rescue lost but with less regret.

On that day, everything baseball had become a hard limit for me. Dad's and my love for all things sports shifted, but at least we still bonded and enjoyed the Pats, Celtics, and Bruins.

"Christine," Dad said when I answered, "Uncle Bradly wanted me to ask if you would be interested in assisting them with a last-minute fundraiser."

A heaviness settled in my chest. Too often, I got caught up in my own little world, forgetting about those who suffered around me. Wanting to live, experiencing freedom because I could, probably made me appear selfish to those outside my bubble. But those inside? They saw my loyalty, that giving nature I lavished on all those in need.

Uncle Bradley wasn't blood, but he'd been beside Dad and me for more of our outdoor sporting events than not when I'd been a kid. They'd gone to school together, attended the same college, married and even had kids within months of each other. Not that I was close with their daughter. She'd had depressive struggles as a child which had blown into suicide attempts and eventually a mental institute.

But I would do anything for Uncle Bradley and Auntie Sophie who both worked for the New England Patriots's organization and had gotten Dad and me season tickets for ten years in a row.

"You know I will," I promised Dad, trusting him to relay

my agreement to whatever it was Uncle Bradley needed my help with.

Dad gave me a quick rundown of what his best friend wanted, and I climbed aboard the idea, ready to take the reins and roll with it. There wasn't a lot of time to get a plan in place, but I was definitely the bitch for the task.

People could trust me to get shit done, and with Uncle Bradley, it wouldn't just be a job but a passion project as well. With his connections, I expected a lot of big names at the event too—definitely a perk.

"I have his number, so I'll give him a call tomorrow before we leave for the game," I promised my dad.

"Are you going out tonight?" he asked, concern lowering his tone.

Unless I babysat for Jessica or went out to dinner with my dad, I always went downtown on the weekends. But, I wasn't about to tell him the truth of who I was meeting up with that night.

"Yep," I answered. "Going dancing."

"Please be careful," Dad said, without a doubt worried that I took my chances during a time of unrest with the whole bombing situation. But I wasn't about to let some homophobic asshole ruin my nightlife.

"Chantelle's Too doesn't allow bags, and they're even making everyone who enters go through metal detectors. I'll be fine," I assured Dad, having checked before suggesting Jarod hook up with me there. "Promise."

"Call me if you need me."

My throat tightened at his request. "I will, Dad." Swallowing hard, I hung up. Like me, Dad would always answer, no matter what time of the day, no matter where he might be or what he did.

"Fuck." Lips in a thin line, I returned to the bathroom to

make sure the wetness welling in my eyes didn't cause my makeup to smear.

Shutting down thoughts of lost love, my mom, and assholes who embraced violence rather than acceptance, I strode back toward my front door. Necessities for the night in hand, I went outside to climb into my waiting Uber.

I could have requested Elite to pick me up with their limo—and meet Jarod exactly as Jessie had done with Reid, but again with the no date-ish feels for the night. It would be hard enough moving on from good dick. I couldn't imagine getting to know the guy first, actually clicking or feeling a connection, then bending over the closest piece of furniture and being fucked until I melted at his feet.

Butterflies erupted inside me as I settled into the backseat of my ride, and restless energy had me squirming. I'd made the mistake of not getting myself off while showering, wanting to save my climaxes for when Jarod stuffed me full, but I was worked up enough with anticipation that another three or four bouts of release in the coming hours would have been easily accomplished.

Especially if he fucked like a god—which he must, right? How else would a guy get hired to be an escort?

My panties were soaked by the time I stood inside the dance club thumping with bass, sex already scenting the air. Slightly on edge, I grabbed a beer and tucked myself into a corner where I could enjoy the coolness sliding down my throat and not draw too much attention.

With curves scantily covered by tight clothes and having long red hair that refused to be tamed, I tended to get a lot of attention when I went out. I didn't need it tonight. Only twenty minutes left until our agreed-upon time to meet up, so I focused on the main entrance, expecting Jarod to be prompt if not early.

Or maybe he'd already arrived in order to do the same of watching for me to arrive.

I quickly scanned the balcony across from where I stood, but the lone pretty boy I looked for scanning the gyrating bodies in front of me wasn't there.

The beer didn't help to lessen my jitters, and I couldn't stay still any longer or I'd lose my ever loving mind. I started moving my hips there at the crowd's edge, keeping in sight of the door. Another song ended without my escort's arrival. Drink downed, I tossed the bottle in the nearest can and allowed myself to get caught up in the sea of lust, the warmth of bodies beckoning to my hormones and my need for release.

Jarod was a professional and knew what I looked like from the picture I'd had to send to Elite. He would find me.

Then he would make my sacrifice of gifting Jessie a night on the town totally worth it.

Thank you in advance, karma.

Chapter 4

Jarod

Thumping music and flashing lights flooded my senses exactly as I expected of the club Christine had requested I meet her at. I glanced over the mass of writhing bodies, too large to find one woman even if my height allowed me to see over quite a bit of the crowd.

Since I'd arrived a few minutes early, I moved toward the bar to get a soda water and waited for service, head and eyes in constant motion searching for the redhead I couldn't wait to see in real life.

"What can I get ya?" The bartender's loud voice pulled me back around.

I leaned forward. "Cranberry and soda water," I half-yelled at the woman wearing a black brassiere, corset-type top to plump up her small breasts.

Her gaze flitted over my wide shoulders and the Henley hugging my pecs. "You got it," she hollered back, a glint in her eyes and a smile on her purple-stained lips while she grabbed a glass.

I angled sideways, checking out the length of the long bar and the thickening group of people wanting attention and something to help get their buzz on. While I would rather down some ice-cold Grey Goose, Elite had a strict policy about liquor. It included a strict two-glass of wine or champagne limit in their employee contract. Condom use and monthly testing were also part of the deal, but getting paid for fucking made the damn rubbers worth it. Sheathing that shit also set aside concerns about knocking some woman up—a major mistake since I had zero interest in bringing any kids into the world.

My luck, they'd end up at the cancer center like Mary Rose had.

There was no trace of Christine at the bar, and I turned back to the bartender when she set my drink down in front of me. I handed a twenty over in exchange for my drink. "Keep the change."

She offered a flirty wink. "Thanks!"

I dipped my head and moved off, heading for the stairs leading to the balcony overhead. Finding a spot by the railing, I sipped my drink and began my perusal of the mass of people humping away below me.

Pure sex in sight, sound, and flashing color, the crowded dance floor enticed even the most stoic to let loose. The swarm of bodies drew focus. Warmed blood. I'd never had issues getting hard, hadn't once needed to pop a little blue pill to get it up for the night job, so the vibe of the club, never mind the promise of Christine, had me at half-mast, ready to go once I was given the green light.

One song morphed into another as the DJ worked his magic, the new slower beat brought a good, slow fuck to mind. Dozens of people with the same thoughts lined the floor beneath me, a handful of threesomes, hips grinding, and mouths fused, wandering hands.

Blonde, brunette, all pairings imaginable...

There.

My mouth dried, and my hand paused half-raised with my drink. Long auburn waves hung halfway down a bared, pale back. She had legs for days ending in heels no woman ought to own the way she did. An ass that could take a pounding and beg for seconds held my stare as I brought my gaze back upward. Lust instantaneously shot through my groin, and I hissed a couple of curses, heat sliding through my veins.

I placed my glass on the nearest table without taking my eyes off of the woman as my hard-on begged for freedom from the confines of my jeans.

Be Christine. Please.

Even if the woman drawing me in like a magnet wasn't my client for the night, I planned on weaving through the crowd to dance with her anyway. I wanted her like I hadn't wanted someone...ever.

And all I'd gotten an eyeful of was her spectacular backside.

She slowly turned, swaying with the music as I descended the stairs, my cock leading the way. Her head lifted, and our gazes met. Clashed. Christine's big green eyes stared straight through my brain, zapping life to every cell in my body and stealing my breath. Her lips parted, and my dick bucked hard in my jeans, pulling a groan from deep in my chest.

Adrenaline rushed, painfully straining my cock against the zipper, and I swallowed a curse while striding down the stairs, desperate to lessen the space between us.

Christine smiled with a *come get me* suggestion in her eyes and shimmied back around, wiggling her fine ass that had my hands clenching, lusting to fill my palms with the soft flesh.

One last tread and I reached the dance floor, moving through dry-humping bodies and a cloud of perfume, aftershave, and sweat. People pressed against me as I weaved through the crowd—female and male alike—but I focused on the glimpse of red hair I kept catching ahead of me.

She turned again, and her green-eyed gaze landed on me.

Ten feet.

Five.

Fucking luscious lips curved and cheeks flushed, she stared at me, her body still swaying like a sex-starved siren, reeling me in.

I grasped her hip, slowly drawing her in. The sweet scent of honeysuckle swarmed my senses like bees, creating havoc in my ears—or perhaps it was the rush of pulsing blood through my arteries as I took in the rest of her gorgeous face.

Perfectly arched auburn eyebrow. Slightly crooked nose. Those goddamn lips that sent need throbbing through my balls. Pointy chin promised stubbornness. Generous cleavage in her slinky top sent my mind toward fucking between the soft flesh. Her nipples pebbled beneath my stare. Wide hips and legs longer than a twelve-hour shift beneath her mid-thigh skirt...Christine was all woman. A teenager's wet dream. A man's fantasy. A perfect specimen for my own spank bank.

Sliding my thigh between hers, I gave her something to grind against. The warmth of her core brushed over my jeans as though no material separated our skin.

I tugged her even closer.

Lifting my gaze revealed the pulse throbbing in her neck and her pupils dominating the green of her eyes. The mutual lust, the same need drawing me closer, making me want to burrow deep inside her and never come up for air, radiated in her stare.

Chemistry between two people was only meant for fairy tales and Hallmark movies over the holidays.

But at that moment, I got it. Fucking felt it down deep in the marrow of my bones. The hairs on my nape rose as images of what could be—what *would* be as soon as I got Christine alone—shot through my mind's eye.

Barely keeping my grasping knuckles from going white on her hip, I spun Christine around, fitting her back perfectly against my body. A few inches shorter than my six-three, her head rested on my shoulder, my straining dick against the top of her ass crack. She rested against my chest, our hips gyrating in perfect rhythm as though we'd been dancing together our whole lives.

I gathered her mass of hair in one fist, tugging to bare her pale neck. Inhaling deeply, I nosed along her smooth skin, salivating over the scent of woman beneath the honeysuckle sweetness.

"You *are* Christine, aren't you?" I didn't doubt my memory of the image Dina had sent me, but Micah would kill me if I took the wrong woman to bed.

"Yes." I barely heard her reply through the beat of the sensual music.

"Thank fuck." I groaned the words against her ear, letting her know how much the sight of her pleased me.

She swayed her hips beneath my hand, grinding her round ass against my hard cock. Moving with her—mimicking a slow, sensual fuck—I licked from her clavicle to her lobe, groaning at her sweet yet slightly salty taste.

A shudder wracked through Christine, and I slid my hand from her hip over her soft belly, my pinkie resting atop her pubis.

"Jesus," she hissed, shifting her lush backside all the fuck over my aching dick.

My groin throbbed, the desperate desire to bury myself balls deep inside of her body driving my swiveling hips. I wanted to devour her whole. Take everything she offered and take it again. Heat rushed through me as I trailed open-mouthed kisses from her neck to her shoulder and back up again, the loud bass coursing through my body with the need to fuck.

Christine arched into me, her arms lifting to grab hold of my neck, and I slid my hand upward, fingers brushing the side of her large breast while I drank in the sight of her cleavage and tight nipples.

I had to adjust my junk. Grip the base to keep from blowing my load like a fresh-faced virgin who'd never gotten to dip his dick into a wet pussy.

Instead, I tightened my hold on her hair with a growl, tipped her head—and laid claim to her mouth.

No soft brushes of lips exchanged between us, simply pure lust, a hunger to delve deeper, taste, and steal breath. Her tongue met mine, stroke for stroke, our bodies shifting in the same vein as though fucking through our clothes.

Electrical sparks zapped through my bloodstream, kicking up my heartbeat when I already felt as though it would burst from my chest. My goddamn head went light as awareness of Christine made its way known through my entire body. A deep yearning to explore, to learn every inch of her, and have her shatter beneath me overwhelmed my brain.

My hand pressed tight to her belly once more, keeping her clasped tight against me—but she wasn't close enough. The thump of the music beat in time with my heart, sending hot blood thrumming through my veins.

How far would she allow me to take things in public? Exhibitionism hadn't been listed as a limit, and with the way she ate at my mouth as I did hers without a care about the press of bodies against us, I expected I could get away with a lot.

She gasped into my mouth but didn't shy from my touch as I cupped her pussy through her skirt. Heat seared my hand, and I cursed. Grinding the heel of my palm against her clit only made her more frantic, her hands grasping at my hair, her cinnamon-laced breath panting between our hovering lips.

She writhed against me, shivering and trembling. "Fucking hell," she spoke over my mouth.

We needed to get out of there before I seriously lost my mind and ended up getting us tossed out for screwing in public. Tearing my lips off hers, I glanced around, wondering what wall I could fuck her against.

A whole arsenal of toys sat in the Elite-provided bag in the limo parked a couple of blocks away, but I wanted her to come undone in my arms.

Sucking her lobe into my mouth, I slid my fingers over the front of her stretchy skirt, mapping out the swell and indent between her thighs. She turned her head, taking my mouth again in a searing, owning kiss, and I rubbed against the hard nub beneath my fingers as she tried to suck the breath from my lungs.

Never one to give a fuck about people watching, I continued to tease her through the thin fabric separating my fingers from her skin. I humped her plump ass in time with the beat, relentless with my fingers to shatter her right there in the middle of the sea of lust surrounding us.

Christine shuddered. "Oh shit...you're gonna make me come."

Fuck yes.

I swallowed her cries as she came, gasping against my mouth, fingernails digging into my wrist as I continued to play with her clit.

"Jesus...." She gasped. Shuddered. Sagged in my arms.

I nuzzled my nose beneath her earlobe again as she panted for breath, eyes closed and smiling.

"Let's get out of here," I stated against her ear, trying to ignore my throbbing balls on the verge of explosion.

Lacing her fingers through mine resting once more atop her hip, she nodded.

When had holding hands felt so...

Fuck, I didn't even know what. Like two puzzle pieces? Made to slot together and instill a sense of rightness I couldn't comprehend—didn't want to.

I turned and pressed through the crowd, Christine in tow. Whatever the fuck was going on between me and my client for the night, I had no clue, but impatience ramped my steps to escape the throng of dancers keeping me from pulling her into privacy where I could ravish every goddamn inch of her deliciousness.

The level of the music prohibited me from excusing us properly, so I shouldered into people when necessary, holding tightly to Christine's slender fingers.

Beneath the balcony by the bar, the noise level lowered a bit, and Christine squeezed my hand. I stopped, pulled her up against my side, and leaned down when she gestured for me to lower my face.

"Bathroom," she said, her raised voice in my ear.

Nodding, I followed where she led.

A long hallway branched off adjacent to the dance floor, the guarded door muffling the music as it closed behind us.

My ears rang, only the low thump of bass still recognizable in the sudden stillness.

Adjusting my aching cock in my jeans, I grimaced. A mess of pre-cum smeared inside my boxer briefs. I couldn't begin to imagine the state of Christina's panties.

A shot of lust kicked me in the groin, and I groaned, squeezing my bulge.

Two women stood in the hallway ahead of us, but the bathroom door in front of them swung inward, spilling out three stumbling, giggling girls. They passed us, and Christine paused, placing her hand against my chest, pushing gently.

I gave way, resting my shoulders against the wall.

"Don't go anywhere," Christine murmured, her emerald eyes reaching through my own dark orbs to seek out every hidden secret inside my soul. "I'm not done with you yet."

She left me, my jaw unhinged and brain fried.

I couldn't even remember my fucking name.

Chapter 5

Christine

Face flushed and my entire body tingling, I entered a stall and shut myself away from the other women inside the bathroom. My cum-soaked panties clung to my pussy, sticky and gross. Too bad I couldn't have snuck Jarrod into the stall with me to lick me clean.

Whimpering a curse, I took care of my full bladder and wiped my panties as free of wetness as I could.

Jarod was so. Damn. Fine. He'd proven to be even hotter in person—and he was mine for the rest of the night.

A shiver of excitement slid down my spine as I washed my hands. I moved on unsteady legs to the full-length mirror, casting a smile at the two women beside me. In typical bitch form, they ignored me while adjusting their boobs. As an only child and having a tomboy for a mother, I never understood women and their cattiness.

Fuck hair highlights and nail appointments. Give me boys, beer, and sports any day of the week.

I might be just like my mom personality-wise, but I sure as hell didn't look like her. I was a spitting image of my dad with his coloring, but even if I chopped my hair and wore overalls, no one would mistake me for anything but a woman.

My breasts felt heavy, my hard nubs aching and sensitive inside the lace contraption keeping them pert and smooshed together. Poking my belly reminded me of the extra I carried around, those damn pounds I'd gained in college and had yet to shed. Turning, I took stock of my bubble butt, then the shapely legs ending in heels that killed my feet.

At least I was hot as shit for the men who liked their women with enough cushion to pound into. Jarod sure as hell hadn't seemed turned off by what he'd seen. And how he'd stalked across the dance floor, dark eyes intent on drinking me down, devouring me as I'd swayed, all but begging him to put his hands on me?

A shuddered sigh ripped through me. My eyes appeared sated. Happy.

And the night hadn't even begun.

While I'd experienced anticipation all day long, Jarod had gone above my expectations. He'd had me so damn revved from the first glance, from the first burning touch of his hand on my hip...I'd felt like I'd been edged until he finally offered relief with talented fingers atop clothing.

Shit. The man hadn't even needed a roadmap. He knew the shortcuts to make me come undone, melt completely beneath his touch. And his mouth?

"Just wow," I murmured, noting my pupils swelling once more. His tongue, the gentle nips of his teeth, had driven my mind to absolute emptiness beyond my need to climax. I couldn't begin to imagine being spread out for him to feast upon.

A pulse shot through my core, and grinning, I turned

away, heels clicking on the tile floor with every confident stride.

I had exactly one night to enjoy the hell out of Jarod's perfection, and I wasn't about to take it easy on him or that hard package between his thick thighs. The poor man wouldn't be able to walk in the morning if I had things my way.

He'd stayed put, right where I'd left him leaning his tall form against the hallway wall. He stood taller than my six feet thanks to my heels. His dark hair was mussed from my grasping hands, mysterious eyes took their time sliding down over me, and his Henley and jeans clung to every bulge lining his muscular body.

Including that monster cock grinding all up on my ass. That bit of flesh was a moneymaker, and I planned to enjoy every second allotted to me.

"See something you like?"

His low voice sent a shiver down my spine, and I cocked an eyebrow while meeting his gaze. "I see something I *want*," I sassed, my tone flirty and full of need.

A groan emitted between his luscious, full lips, and he reached for me. "Give me your hand, woman."

Normally, I didn't follow orders, but I moved on autopilot as though recognizing the daddy in Jarod. Not that I needed or wanted one. But for that night? I would indulge in the fantasy by submitting a little bit.

I laced my fingers with his again, loving how well our palms fit together. He had big hands. Talented fingers. Wetness dripped from my pussy, soaking my panties again. He hadn't even touched the skin between my legs, and I'd come harder than I had in years.

It was no wonder the man was one of Elite's most sought-after escorts. While there was no such thing as a perfect man outside of smut books, Jarod Zimmerman had to that point clicked all my buttons. I'd never felt so drawn to a man, never experienced an overwhelming need to wrap my body around a guy and beg him to stay until morning. I didn't even know Jarod, but I wouldn't mind opening my eyes every morning to the sight of his bedhead and that mouth tasting mine.

Insta-lust lived like a magnet between us. Thank fuck I didn't believe in insta-*love*. And thank fuck both our hearts weren't on the table, or there would have been trouble for sure.

Jarod led me into the ruckus of the club, but seconds later, we stepped out into the early evening. Boston's downtown was alight with passing cars and the roar of a plane taking off from Logan sounded from beyond our sight. A few horns honked, adding to the noise, but an elderly lady hobbled past us, gaining my attention. She appeared as though she needed a cane to help steady her steps, and I glanced around to see if anyone accompanied her.

Jarod tucked me in close, pulling my mind back to his holy hotness before I could offer assistance. I fit perfectly against him without having to slouch. Pleasure rippled through me, snagging my full focus. I was no petite woman in need of a man's protection, but at that moment, I relished the feeling of a bigger man's arm slung around my shoulders.

Although exhaust and the salt of the ocean clung to the air surrounding us, I filled my lungs with the scent of his cologne—citrus and spice.

My mouth watered.

"You're in charge, Christine. Where are we off to?" His words stirred the hair by my ear, and I sucked in a sharp breath as he bit my earlobe. In charge, my ass. I had a say in where we would go, but I expected that might be it when it came to the man keeping me close against his side.

On a normal night, I would have headed for a sports bar to catch the day's highlights while downing a few beers, but our time was limited. "My place."

I'd just bought my own home and that un-christened king-sized bed I'd splurged on? Jarod was definitely the man for the job.

"Did you drive?" he asked, his hand dropping to my hip and tugging me tighter against him.

"Uber." I tilted up my head to take in his gorgeous cheekbones and tasty, full lips. "Reid had a limo when he'd picked up Jessie, so I assumed..." I shrugged.

His slow smile sent another rush of arousal through my core. "Not a problem." He fished a phone from his back pocket and without releasing his hold on me, texted with one hand.

I once more took note of the old woman who stood alongside the curb. Pulling away from Jarod, I approached her. "Can I walk you across the street?"

She smiled and patted my arm. "Thank you, honey, but I'm just waiting for my cab."

Nodding, I returned to Jarod who shoved his phone away again.

He glanced at the woman then me, eyes thoughtful.

"So, you like to dance?" he asked, rather than question my interaction with the older woman..

"I'm not the best dancer but—"

"You move like pure passion drenched in sin."

I grinned. "I enjoy the writhing masses. The scent of sex in the air as people try to fuck through clothing. It's a complete turn-on. Makes me wet."

He blinked as though surprised by my candid words

and pressed down on the ridge of the undeniable hard-on beneath his jeans. "Fuck, the way you talk."

I purred, so damn ready to drive him past caring where we fucked. While I wasn't in the mood to get tossed into the slammer for indecent exposure, I wasn't above giving at least the limo driver a good show.

"You like to fuck." Jarod didn't voice a question.

"I'm a woman. I like men. I love the hardness of a male body against mine and chasing the high of a good orgasm."

"How do you like it?"

"Sex?"

He nodded.

"Any and all ways." I glanced at the long line still waiting for admittance to Chantelle's Too, Boston's newest dance club we'd enjoyed perhaps a bit too much past the point of prudent, but I didn't really give a fuck. The owner was the same Chantelle who supposedly owned a club of other sorts too—the whips and chains type. Not my bag exactly, but to each their own.

"I let my mood dictate though." I glanced up into Jarod's dark eyes.

Warm and open, those orbs peered down at me, a hint of a smile ghosting on his lips. "And tonight?" he asked, angling his body, giving me a very good feel along my hip of what he had on offer.

My pussy spasmed at the thought of him sliding into my core. Wrecking me. "Well, since you *are* a professional, I'm expecting at least two if not three rounds of the best sex of my life." I sounded like a needy whore but put the blame on him in my mind.

"Is that a fact?"

"Mmm." I slid my hand down his throat and over the

swell of his rock-hard pecs. "First one hard and fast—wall, table, island in my kitchen—you can take your pick."

"I like the way you think."

God. The gravel in his voice...I clenched my thighs together. "The second, I want it slow. So damn slow you have me begging for release, all the while denying me."

That ghostly smile hinted to life again. "And the third?"

"If you're up for it—" I wormed my hand between us and grabbed hold of his impressive girth "—I'll let you choose."

A limo pulled up to the curb beside us, and I squeezed Jarod through his jeans before releasing my grip on his cock.

"As you wish," he whispered against my lips but pulled back before actually kissing me.

Flushed through with heat and the need for another orgasm, I climbed into the car after a quick thanks to the chauffeur, whose hair was slicked-back into a ponytail.

"Thanks, Ricky," Jarod said from behind me.

Cool leather kissed the back of my thighs as I slid onto the seat and scooted over to make room for him. With enough seating for eight, the limo was spacious enough for a good hard fuck. I should have told him I didn't want to wait until we got to my place for that first wild ride.

I noted a black duffle on the floor and wondered at the toys and sex paraphernalia inside. Reid had the same Elite-provided bag on his and Jessica's date—or so I'd been told, but all he'd used was the massage oil.

Jarod lowered onto the seat beside me and pressed close, his large hand grasping the top of my thigh.

"Where to?" Ricky asked as he settled behind the wheel a moment later.

I spouted off my address quite a ways up Route 1, and with a nod, he shut the window between us, encasing Jarod and me in complete privacy. Soft music came to life, and seconds later, the limo pulled out into Boston's nighttime traffic.

"For the first fuck, I'm going to take you against the front door of your house, but right now," Jarod said, lowering to his knees in front of me, "I'm going to bury my nose between these thighs and lick your sweet pussy until you squirm."

"I like the way *you* think," I echoed his earlier words, my voice breathless, betraying my body's need.

His hands slid up my thighs, pushing my skirt into a bunch. I wiggled, assisting in his plan, and he yanked me to the seat's edge.

"Comfy?" he asked, trailing a fingertip against the soaked silk covering me.

"Comfy enough. Now, blow my mind."

Jarod made a low growly sound. "It'll be my pleasure."

Chapter 6

Jarod

I hooked my fingers under the sides of Christine's panties and pulled them down her long, shapely legs, releasing her heeled feet one at a time. The scent of honeysuckle and her arousal swarmed the air around me, making my mouth water.

Tossing the panties aside, I grasped her knees, spreading her legs wide.

A low groan rose in my chest over the trimmed red hairs atop her pubis. A lot of men loved the bare look, but I'd always had a thing for the appearance of maturity. Fucking loved the musky scent that clung between a woman's thighs too.

"So pretty." I thumbed over her mound and leaned in, nosing along her curves. Her need flooded my senses, and I breathed in deeply.

Christine muttered something about me being an animal while threading her fingers through my hair.

I grunted in agreement and licked up through her tangy wetness.

Delicious.

Glancing upward with my second stroke, I found Christine's eyes shut, her head tipped back. Settling in to eat her out until she creamed all over my chin, I gladly went to work. Tongue, nose, and teeth, I didn't fuck around, but I tortured her with my lust to taste every inch of her soft petals before latching onto her clit.

Christine ground against my face, chasing her orgasm, but I released my suction and dipped low once more, trailing the tip of my tongue over her hole and beneath, searching out her tight pucker.

"Oh, God." She gulped as I rimmed her ass, softening the flesh until I could probe inside without difficulty.

Humming my approval at her body's submission to my tongue, I lapped back up to her clit, nipping and suckling until she panted, writhing against my hold on her spread thighs.

"Jarod," she breathed, her raspy tone a kick of lust to my tight balls.

"Mmm," I hummed against her clit and descended once more to keep her on the edge.

"Goddamnit!" She yanked on my hair as I roamed southward with a snicker. Blinking open passion-hazed eyes, she caught my gaze. Her grasp tightened on my hair. "Please. I need to come."

Leaning back, I licked her arousal from my lips and pressed two fingers into her soaked core. We both let out a moan, and my dick throbbed, desperate to bury in her slick heat.

"Is this what you need, Christine?" Still holding her gaze, I flicked my tongue over her protruding nub while slowly pumping into her body. "My fingers fucking your pussy and my mouth on your clit?"

"Oh, fuck." Her head tipped back again as I latched

onto her thickened nub. "Don't stop. Please...Christ, don't stop!"

Nothing better than a begging woman shuddering beneath your touch. Continuing to suckle, I twisted my wrist, pushing deeper, fingertips rubbing...searching.

She jolted—bingo.

Teasing the hell out of her G, I lapped at her clit until she shuddered, her panted breaths closing in on a whine.

"Give it to me." I flicked my tongue over her nub and rubbed deep inside her.

Christine released with a gasped cry, her core clamping down and creaming all over my fingers.

Fuck yes.

Wet squelching noises—lewd and indecently arousing—pulsed need through my groin, and I groaned while lapping up her cum.

A shudder rippled down through Christine, and I eased from devouring to gentle strokes of both fingers and tongue. Once she slumped, I pulled free, sucking the sweetness of her off my hand.

Humming over her addictive flavor, I watched her fluttering eyelashes, her parted lips. Drank in the flush over her freckled cheeks and the pulse thrumming in her neck.

"Holy shit," she breathed, her mouth curling upward. "It's no wonder you get paid to please a woman."

Grinning, I kissed each of her thighs and tugged her skirt back down a bit.

"It's easy when said woman tastes like heaven." I didn't lie while settling once more onto the seat beside her. "I could eat you out ten times a day and still crave more."

A shudder rippled through her at my statement. She blinked open hazed eyes.

My heart skipped a beat as her gaze landed on mine.

Same as the second I'd first caught sight of those emerald orbs, I found myself wanting to lean in and drown in her focus. Lose myself to whatever witchery she brewed inside her.

Clearing my throat, I forced my focus on the mini-bar. "Drink?"

"Got any beer?" she asked, her voice a little scratchy.

"Sure thing."

I popped the top off a longneck and handed it over, the simple graze of our fingers sending a shockwave through me.

Ignoring how she tilted the bottle up, swallowing down the cool beverage, I retrieved her panties from the floor.

"Want these back?" I asked, lifting the soaked bit of satin.

She swallowed her beer before answering. "That depends."

"On?"

"If you have a treasure full of hoarded panties at home."

I didn't—but I suddenly felt the desire to hide hers away from anyone else. Where only I had access to bury my nose in them. Sniff and fill my lungs with her musky sweetness.

They were mine, and I *wasn't* giving them back.

Pre-cum oozed from my slit, and grinning, I stuffed a client's panties in my jeans pocket for the first time since signing on with Elite.

She huffed a little snort. "Guess that answers that question."

I didn't bother correcting her about my lack of having a secret stash of cum-covered panties at home. Instead, I opened a bottle of cold water and sucked it down, hoping to cool my dick off the edge of desire to drive into her warmth.

"So how'd you come to work for Elite?" she asked and swigged from her beer again.

Usually, I hated the small talk, the needless and unwanted chatter to pass slower moments while on the clock. But with Christine? I settled in for the ride, wanting whatever I could get out of her. I expected the conversation wouldn't be stilted or feel forced. Our bodies definitely had an ease between them, and I figured our minds would as well.

"My good friend owns the business," I answered.

"Get out."

"Nope. He started the professional escort business years ago. When money got tight and tuition went up, I needed to supplement my income. Being eye candy and loaning out my dick seemed like a better side job than stocking grocery shelves."

She snickered, her focus steady on my face without a hint of embarrassment or judgment, which I happened to see a lot even though the clients hired me for the night. "Does it ever get old?"

I hesitated in answering. "Not *old*. Some days it does feel like a chore though since I'm not always in the mood to socialize."

"So, you called this your side job—what do you do during the day? Or is personal stuff off-limits in case clients get all stalkerish on your ass?"

A huff of laughter escaped me at her question. While I usually didn't discuss my life with anyone outside my small bubble of friends, Christine was...different. Like I'd simply gone to a club and picked her up on my own with no money exchanged, no contracts signed.

"I'm a nurse," I answered truthfully, not sure how to feel about the draw between us. The undeniable attraction seemed like more than a hookup would have been back in the day when I'd needed to find my own pussy.

Her eyebrows popped up in surprise at my answer. "You seem more the macho sports-type than compassionate caregiver."

"I'm all about sports, but I had leukemia when I was a kid—"

"Oh, God."

"—and I adored the nurses who helped me fight it." I shrugged, somehow knowing she would get why I'd chosen the career path I had.

Her gaze softened, a display of compassion that warmed my chest. "I can see how that would be a huge influence."

"My parents split just a few months after I'd started treatments, and the stability of the hospital and its staff became more of a home than the two I ended up bouncing between." Words kept spilling from my mouth, and I didn't bother trying to police them.

"That must have sucked ass."

"It did." I reached out and twirled one of her long waves of hair through my fingers before sipping my water again. "Made me feel responsible, you know?"

"You weren't."

I nodded, having told myself that exact thing a thousand times, but shit still lingered in my conscience sometimes.

"So no relapses?" she asked.

"Nope." I shook my head. "I've had a clean bill of health since I was twelve."

"Are your parents still around?"

"Both of them. Dad lives on the South Shore, Mom's down the Cape."

She lifted her beer, fully focused on my face. "Where do you call home?"

"Now that *is* a little too personal."

She smirked at my teasing tone. "Afraid I'm going to get all weird on your ass and start following you around?"

"Nah. You aren't the needy, unstable type."

"Oh?" Christine lifted one auburn eyebrow in a sexy quirk. "Have me all figured out after gifting me two orgasms, do you?"

I shrugged, my focus slipping down to her smirking lips I wanted to taste again. "I like to think I'm pretty good at reading people."

"All right, then." She angled on the seat to face me, her skirt riding up in the process and drawing my gaze down to the length of thigh she flashed. "What have you concluded about me?"

"You're confident. Aggressive. You know what you want and you speak your mind."

A light laugh escaped her. "Anyone would be aware of those facts within two minutes of meeting me."

"You're empathetic and compassionate. Giving."

She narrowed her gaze. "You've been talking to Reid."

"Nope."

"But you're aware I paid for his night with Jessica."

"I didn't need to know that to see the softness in your eyes when that elderly woman shuffled past us on the sidewalk."

Her eyebrows furrowed, eyes growing a bit stormy— concerned. "She shouldn't have been out walking alone like that even if she was just waiting for a cab."

"Agreed."

Christine finished off her beer, and I took the empty bottle from her. "I'm not looking forward to getting old," she murmured.

"You're not a vain person," I stated what I'd also learned about Christine in our short time together.

Her eyebrow shot up again as though surprised by my assumption. "It's more the frailty and being unable to care for myself is what I can't stand the thought of."

"I think most people feel that way," I murmured, setting her bottle aside.

"God." She grimaced and glanced out the window as Ricky eased off the gas and entered the ramp taking us off Route 1. "Enough of the morbid. Talk dirty to me."

That, I could definitely do.

Chapter 7

Christine

Jarod's hot breath ghosted over my ear as he gathered my hair up, gently tucking the heavy mass around my shoulder, out of his way. Once more inhaling like an animal, he ran his nose along my neck as though desperate to draw my scent deep into his lungs.

"You smell sweet like honeysuckle."

A shiver raised the hairs on my arms, and I tilted my head, my eyelids fluttering closed. "And you smell like my pussy."

He chuckled and made an appreciative noise under his breath. Neck kisses followed, gentle nips of his teeth grazing over my sensitive skin. Quiet moans rumbled in his chest as he feasted on my throat.

The man was absolutely divine, talented in ways I'd never experienced.

He made me weak, and I sagged against the seat as Jarod's mouth once more found my ear.

"You're infectious," he murmured, sending another scuttle of rising bumps across my forearms. Tugging my legs, he shifted me until I half sat on his lap. "All this silky skin..." Fingertips trailed over my knee and upward to toy with the edge of my skirt. "And freckles." He touched a few of the hundreds scattered over my thigh. "Fucking hell, woman, you're sexy as sin. Can't wait to have your long legs wrapped around my back."

I let out a moan, shuddering as he sucked my lobe between his lips.

"I'll sink into your tight heat. Fill you up. Make you scream and come on my dick."

"Oh, God." I gulped. "Stop, or I'm going to leave a wet spot on your jeans."

"Mmm." He groaned, his exhale hot in my ear. "Another article of clothing for me to sniff later while I'm jerking off to fantasies about owning your body again."

Shit, the man fucking slayed me—and he wasn't even touching me except for that small circle he drew on my thigh with a single fingertip and the soft blush of his lips over my lobe while speaking. "You're dangerous," I whispered, not having intended to let the thought fly.

"Mmm." He nosed along my neck again.

"Fucking hell, Jarod." I whined my response, ready to sink into a puddle of want. I'd never known such chemistry. All those mouths that had come before him, every whispered word of lust I'd heard before had never taken me to the edge of desperation. And I'd already climaxed twice in the past hour.

He was a professional. An escort. Fucked for cash.

It would be good to remember those truths so the romantic side of me I'd buried tight as a teenager didn't rear her sad head beneath the onslaught of everything Jarod.

He spoke to all his clients that way, I told myself. Touched them as he had me. Promised to satisfy.

Ignoring the words in my head didn't come easily. They clung, heavy and dark—

He pulled back enough that I opened my eyes, blessedly giving my racing mind rest. His almost black orbs studied my face as though memorizing every inch, every freckle on my face, every beginning of what I feared were wrinkles at the corners of my eyes. Cradling my head in his hands, he held me still, our heavy breaths filling the back of the limo that had seemed so spacious when we'd first climbed in.

The area closed in on us, shrinking until all I saw was his eyes that appeared ravenous with want.

"Give me your mouth," he murmured, and being the dick-hungry whore I was, I obeyed like a good little girl.

I grabbed two handfuls of his shirt, our lips in no hurry to taste the other's. Inhaling his exhales, I attempted to draw him in deeper, loving how he moaned while exploring along my tongue. His mouth was utter perfection, his kisses drugging. Thought-shattering.

His hand trailed up to my hip, along my side, until he grazed over the side of my breast. My nipples hardened into points, and I shifted, wanting his fingers to tug on them, maybe pinch with a bit of pain.

"Please," I whimpered, resting my forehead against his cheekbone because I couldn't take any more of his mouth that was laying waste to my sense of self-preservation.

Jarod slid his hand beneath my shirt, tugged the cup of my bra down, and palmed my hot flesh. He made a noise of enjoyment, tightening his hold around my back to keep me pressed against him as best he could on the leather seat. "So warm and soft...but this..." He thumbed over my nipple. "You're hard and aching for my teeth."

"God, yes," I hissed, arching into his touch, my head tipping away from his.

He slid his hand up my back, grasping at my hair, his mouth once more finding my neck. "Want to suck a bruise right here," he growled, teeth nipping over my throbbing artery.

"Do it."

Chuckling, he pinched my nipple instead.

"Fuck!" I gasped, my core pulsing with need.

"Soon," Jarod murmured, sliding his lips up my neck, over my chin, and once more taking my mouth.

Forget the unhurried tasting from before. Jarod dove in to feed, licking into my mouth, groaning, and rolling my tight nub between his fingers. I squirmed, rubbed my thighs together, sure I could get off from nipple play alone for the first time ever.

It was like the man knew my wiring, knew how to turn me on as easily as a new faucet, knew how to make me beg.

"Please."

"Please what?"

"Need to come," I whined, realizing I'd grabbed his hair and practically pulled the strands free from his scalp.

"Soon, sweet girl."

Oh, God... I'd never been called that—ever.

I liked it too damn much, my insides purring, my entire body shivering.

"But first I want to taste every inch of you. Lick..." He dragged his tongue over the seam of my mouth. "Suck," he murmured before doing that very thing to my lower lip. " Bite." Sharp teeth clamped down on my slick flesh.

Releasing my fingers from his hair, I snaked a hand between us to grab his hard dick. "Want this," I stated while he continued to nibble.

Jarod groaned and released his teeth's hold. "And my cock wants to be shoved so far up your creamy pussy that I forget everything but the feeling of your tightness squeezing me, milking every last drop of cum from my balls."

Fuck, Jarod had dirty talk game in spades. How the hell was I going to survive what we'd already done—and we hadn't even gotten to the good stuff?

The limo slowed, and I blinked, glancing out the tinted window and taking note we'd arrived at my street. "We're here."

Jarod slid my bra back up over my breast before removing his hand from beneath my shirt. He didn't wait for the driver but grabbed the black bag off the floor and opened the door.

Ricky rounded the front of the car as Jarod climbed from the limo and offered me his hand.

Electrical pulses raced through my body as our palms connected.

A crooked grin tilted his lips.

"Want me to wait?" Ricky asked Jarod quietly as I climbed from the limo onto shaking legs, my focus on my escort's flushed appearance.

"Don't bother," he murmured a reply to Ricky but didn't take his eyes off me.

He planned on staying for an extended time, which was fine by me.

Focused on not falling on my face, I started toward my front stairs. My hand still clutched at Jarod's, but he didn't make me drag his ass behind me. He moved with purpose, the same as I did, as though driven by the same desire coursing through me.

My front door—that was where I wanted to be taken first. Held up. Fucked within an inch of my life.

I bit my lip to keep from whimpering.

"Have a good evening," Ricky called out from behind us, a smile in his voice.

"Oh, we will," Jarod answered before I could even think to open my mouth. "Thanks for the ride."

The driver's chuckle followed us up the short walk to my house.

Chapter 8

Jarod

Fingers still clamped around mine, Christine led me up her cobbled path while I grimaced over the discomfort of my throbbing length confined in my jeans. Kind of made for bow-legged walking.

I followed her swaying ass up the three stairs, waiting impatiently for her to unlock her door. The click couldn't come fast enough.

Face a glorious shade of pink, Christine smiled over her shoulder at me, emerald eyes damn near overtaken by her blown pupils. "Ready for round one?" she asked as the lock disengaged, her raspy voice making my dick flex.

Fuck, this woman...

"I've been ready since the second I saw you humping the air on that dance floor." I followed Christine into her foyer and dropped the black bag to the floor.

While she kicked off her heels and set her things on a small side table, I fished the conveniently stashed condom from my back pocket, unzipped my fly, and sheathed my cock in record time.

She flicked on a light, and without a word, I grabbed

and spun her in my arms, our mouths colliding once more. Cinnamon and hops sweetened her breath, and I couldn't swallow her down fast enough. Christine wasn't a small woman, but I had no difficulty grabbing the fleshy globes beneath her skirt and lifting her. She wrapped her legs around my waist, fitting like a goddamned glove, like she belonged plastered against my body. My dick pressed against her clit, so I lifted her higher...and slammed her against her front door while sinking balls deep inside her slick heat.

She ripped her mouth from mine and arched her back, thrusting her tits in my face. "Fuck!"

"Shit yeah," I groaned, taking a brief second to appreciate her tight choke hold on my cock.

Hard and fast, she'd said.

Arms in a vise around her soft curves, I pulled out and rammed in, my mouth latching onto the top of the jiggling flesh of her cleavage. I bit with enough force to leave indents. Sucked with the intent of bruising her skin in a place she could easily hide.

"You feel so fucking good, Christine." I growled and licked up her neck, the sweet scent of honeysuckle coating the back of my throat and nose. "So. Fucking. Good." I grunted each word with a thrust as my fingertips dug into her ass cheeks.

The sounds of wet fucking and gasping breaths accompanied the slap of our bodies coming together. Every stab of my cock deep inside her core gifted me a grunt from her parted lips. Curses. Moans. She grasped at my hair, yanking to the point of pain, but I didn't give a fuck. She was like heaven wrapped around me, and a bald patch or two would be worth the climax building in my balls.

She groaned, head tipped back and eyelids clenched shut. "Harder. Yes. Fuck, you're going to wreck me."

I bent my knees slightly, snapping my hips higher.

"Fuck!" Christine shrieked. "Right fucking there. Oh God..."

"Like that, do you?" I lusted to go deeper, on the verge of losing it as her legs squeezed my waist, trying to meld me into her body. "My dick all up in your needy pussy?"

"Fuck, yes! Give it to me." She panted, and I stared, memorizing every freckle across her nose, turned on by the furrow between her eyebrows, the intensity with which she enjoyed being impaled by my rock-hard length.

My hips moved on their own accord in my need to split her in half. "Want you to come on my dick, sweet girl. Need your cum dripping off my balls."

"Oh, shit." Whimpering, she smashed her mouth into mine, teeth clashing and tongues dueling as our bodies slammed together. A whined moan started deep in her chest, and she gasped twice against my lips before she convulsed. "Jarod!"

Her inner walls clamped on my girth like a pulsing fist, her juicy cum dripping down over my groin just like I'd wanted.

"Christ." The word tore from my lips as my climax roared through my body, my cum spurting into the condom with every erratic thrust of my hips. "Jesus...fuck, Christine," I growled the words on my last thrust, burying deep and clinging to her relaxed softness.

We gasped for breath, our foreheads resting against each other as the last spasm rocked my body, and I shuddered against her.

"Fucking fantastic." Christine moaned and squeezed her inner muscles around my softening length again.

My abs jerked at my oversensitive dick, and I cursed, needing to be free of her body yet wanting to stay put forever.

"Goddamn, woman." I brushed my dry lips over hers, tonguing my way between to lick inside her mouth. Addictively sweet, she made me desire more.

So much *fucking* more...

Christine sighed against my mouth, and I pulled away, finally meeting her gaze. Satiated orbs overtaken once more by green drank in my soul like I was a free glass of water with no other purpose other than to satisfy her needs.

I should have felt used...but didn't, my hips still pinning her against the wall.

My hands found their way into her lush hair, and I pushed the mass back over her shoulders, tucking some other stray strands behind her ears. I realized a small smile curved my lips as I ran a thumb over her cheekbones and the freckles that appeared to map out a picture for me to connect the dots.

Why did being inside her feel so damn good? It hadn't just been the fucking, the release. Even fast and hard, being offered the gift of her body had felt...intimate. Perhaps even tender?

A shiver rippled down my spine—

"You are one fantastic fuck," she murmured and smiled like a lazy, untamable cat.

Pride swelled inside my chest, easing my strange unrest at that moment, but my softening length suggested I ease from her core and set things right.

"You okay?" I asked while pulling free and stepping back enough for her legs to slide to the floor.

She grinned a mischievous curl of lips and flashing white teeth. "Seriously, never better. Want a beer?"

I blinked at her flippant tone. Hadn't she come as hard as I? Weren't her knees a little weak, her body still tingling and wanting to collapse in on itself? "Yeah," I heard myself murmur an answer.

Shimmying her skirt back down her thighs, she stepped around me as though she hadn't just gotten fulfillment from that first round and was left wet and sated. "Bathroom's at the end of the hall."

My gaze glued to her round ass while I yanked my jeans back up from my ankles just high enough I wouldn't trip while making my way to the bathroom. I *definitely* wouldn't have to worry about her getting all clingy or cuddly like some clients, I thought as she opened the fridge as though on a mission. A frown furrowed my brow at her seemingly unfazed attitude by our shared climax that had tilted me completely off-balance. Unsure of what riled inside me, I headed to the bathroom to unsheathe my flaccid dick and clean up.

I'd never enjoyed pleasing a client so much. Hadn't ever gotten so involved in my own headspace and chasing satisfaction that I took rather than gave of myself.

But those curves. That mouth. The sounds she'd made while creaming the hell out of my cock.

A shudder ripped through me, life once more returning between my thighs. Rocking a semi, I returned to the kitchen, determined to figure out what the hell had just happened.

Christine handed me a bottle of Sam Adam's, her gaze flitting over my face. "Are you okay?"

I forced my eyebrows to relax, not having realized I still frowned. "Yeah."

Her dazzling smile hit me like a shot of adrenaline straight to the heart, and I stared as she sashayed into the living room and bent to retrieve the clicker from the coffee table.

I couldn't take my hungry eyes off her, the same as when I'd first caught sight of that spill of red waves hanging down her back.

Lifting the cold bottle, I acknowledged to myself that I needed to clear my head. The hoppy, bitter brew slid down my throat, refreshing as hell and clearing some of the strangeness from my brain. "Damn, I needed that."

"Nothing better than a cold beer after a hot fuck." She tossed a flirty wink over her shoulder before sitting on the couch.

The things that came out of her mouth. I'd never met such an uninhibited vixen, and I swore witchery was at play with how she stirred me up inside like a bubbling cauldron ready to spill over.

"You just gonna stand there all night?" she called to me.

Put one foot in front of the other, I coaxed myself as a sports announcer started in on the day's highlights.

Reality settled over me, and I blinked fully into the present. I'd read Christine's file but hadn't actually thought a woman would be that much into sports she'd enjoy watching a nighttime talk show about them. Especially while sucking down a beer.

"Are you shitting me?" I asked, collapsing onto the couch beside her.

"What?"

I lifted my bottle and pointed to the TV.

"Two of my favorite pastimes." She sipped from her drink, her swollen lips kissing the rim and drawing my focus.

"Are you for real?" I heard myself ask.

Christine flicked her gaze to the wide flatscreen hanging on the wall across from us. "Nope."

Her profile held my attention, and I ignored the drone of the announcer's voice. Barely any makeup painted her face, allowing the darker star-like spots across the bridge of her nose and cheekbones to stand out and demand appreciation. Naturally shaped eyebrows, auburn in color arched over her eyes without a hint of that fake line shit. Pink still flushed her cheeks, and moisture glistened on her full bee-stung lips.

"Goddamnit." Christine scowled.

"What?" I glanced at the screen, realizing I'd been staring in awe-like stupidity at her.

"Jackson *definitely* won't be ready for tomorrow's game."

The Pats's rookie...right. "They told us that late last night," I said, once more lifting my beer and forcing my attention on the update on the Pats's lineup for their game against the Steelers the following afternoon.

"A girl can hope, though," Christine murmured, totally caught up in the host's words. "It's going to be a tough game. Pittsburgh has the same undefeated pre-season record as us."

"3-0," we both said at the same time.

Christine cast a smile my way, and goddamn, did I feel like the sun shone down from the heavens, shooting beams of heat through every cell in my body.

"You're beautiful." I heard myself say the only thought in my head.

"So are you."

My own smile twisted. "I've never been called beautiful before."

"Oh, please." She ran a hand through my hair she'd

messed up and down along my jaw. Staying still rather than leaning into her caress like a needy kid didn't come easy. Her fingertips traced my lips before dropping back to her lap. "I've never seen a prettier man. God created Colin Farrell, tweaked a few things, and made pure perfection with you. I'm sure he had no choice but to crush that mold once you emerged."

I chuckled and took a deep pull of my beer, needing the coolness to release some of the warmth Christine flared inside me. "You're funny."

"It's true."

My lingering smile faded as did hers, our gazes locked. A buzz started up in my ears, or maybe it was simply the heightened pulse of my heart rushing blood through me. Couldn't look away.

"You are so fucking hot it's sinful," Christine murmured, her focus on my mouth. "No man has ever made me come that hard. Shit." She huffed a small laugh, glittering eyes lifting to mine once more and stealing my breath. "My legs almost gave out when you set me back down."

I aimed to please, but I hadn't noticed she'd been that unsteady while my body had been reeling from the climax of a lifetime. "You seemed to stroll away from it without any difficulty." Could I sound any more pouty? I didn't do that shit—ever. But knowing she'd been off-kilter too? That sent blood to pool in my groin, making me needy as fuck. I wanted another go-round with the siren reeling me into the type of high that came along with the possibility of danger. Pain. My thickening dick didn't give two shits about the unease curling in the base of my spine.

I needed more.

She snorted and tipped her beer up for a swig. "I am

master of my body and rarely let people see what's going on inside me."

"You're not shy with your words, but you're definitely a challenge."

Light laughter jiggled those lush tits I imagined thrusting between, making lust pulse through my balls and putting all else from my mind. "I have been called that, yes."

"You know what I think?" I grazed my knuckles over the swell of her breasts, featherlight and teasing.

She swallowed another mouthful of beer but kept her focus glued to my face. "Hmm?"

I put my beer on the coffee table, took hers from her hand, and placed it beside mine. "I think I'm up for it. Gonna make you beg for my dick, sweet girl."

Christine huffed, her emerald eyes glinting as I stood to loom over her. "I've never begged to be fucked. Never will."

"We'll see about that."

Her gaze slid down over my body, resting on the bulge in my jeans. She licked her lip. "Ready to go again already?"

She'd already confessed to lusting for my dick, but I wanted her undone beneath me, overcome by need.

"I could stay hard for you all night long."

Chapter 9

Christine

The heat in his gaze swept through my blood like a brush fire, lighting up every inch of my body with arousal. My smile faded, and I swallowed.

So. Damn. Dangerous.

But it seemed I had zero self-control, no self-preservation left intact—

Jarod tugged me off the couch and bent, lifting me into his arms as though I weighed no more than a twenty-pound dumbbell.

I half-assed smacked at his shoulder. "You're going to throw your back out."

"Hardly."

His snorted reply only made me hotter for him.

He strode across the living room as I ran my hand over his rock-hard pecs, thoughts of round two flicking through my brain. Slow, until I begged, I had requested. God, would I seriously survive this man? Probably not, but I would get my money's worth and have memories to last a lifetime.

"Seriously, put me down before you hurt yourself," I

muttered. What I'd meant was he would hurt *me* by being all romantic and shit.

"Christine, the last thing you are is heavy."

I pressed my lips tight rather than arguing. The "freshman ten" or so I'd gained in my college years had turned into twenty and still clung like a stubborn bitch in all the wrong places. It seemed every couple of weeks, no matter how much bunny food I did or didn't eat, another sixteen ounces found their way to my thighs or breasts.

"You've got the curves of a goddess," he said, his voice low and sexy, "and I'm going to take my time exploring and lavishing attention on every one of them until your mind is quiet. You're going to plead for my dick, then I'll leave you a puddle of sated flesh sprawled out beneath me."

His words shut up every thought in my head, regardless of his reminding me of our non-bet about the whole begging thing. My chest tightened, and I forced myself to focus on his body. Sweaty, torturous sex. The orgasm sure to eventually rip through me. God, did I want him—but I would never lower myself by whining for his length to fill me up again. Harder, yes, but never to stick it in.

Call me stubborn, but I wouldn't ever ask a man for anything let alone beg for his dick, no matter how well he definitely used it.

I nipped his jaw, my tongue drawing lazy circles down his neck as I breathed in his subtle, spicy cologne. He would find a sopping mess between my thighs, and I couldn't wait to see how he would play the game.

Soft and gentle, he laid me on my bed like I was a precious treasure. Ignoring the sweet care I might enjoy a little too much, I propped on my elbows as he peeled off his shirt. My mouth dried and then flooded almost immediately with drool. Wide shoulders and the thick pecs I'd caressed rippled with muscles down toward his washboard abs, and the luscious V at his waist caused my tongue to twitch between my parted lips.

"Fuck me," I breathed, my fingers itching to touch every inch of his gorgeous body.

"Begging already?" he asked, an eyebrow cocked.

I narrowed my gaze in a fake glower.

Chuckling, he dropped his shirt to the floor. "I'll take you there, Christine. Promise." The gravel in his low tone pulsed my core with the desire to be defiled in every way imaginable.

I felt the heat of his stare on my face but couldn't tear mine from his fingers as they flicked open his button and pushed his jeans down. His dick was hard, thick, and ready to fuck, just the way I liked them. I reached for him.

Jarod captured my hand before I could stroke his length. "Maybe later," he said, releasing his hold and grasping the edges of my blouse.

By habit, I sucked in my stomach as he lifted the material over my head, baring my flabby belly. Laying down always flattened everything out—except for my huge breasts that threatened to take up residence in my armpits.

He slipped his fingers beneath the waistband of my skirt, and I lifted my hips as he pulled.

"You're so fucking delightful."

I snorted with laughter at his murmur that sounded a little too...honest. "Who the hell says delightful?"

His dark gaze captured mine, tightening my chest again.

Wariness crept around the edges of my conscience, and I visualized locking my heart up behind ten feet of steel against the smooth words he spewed.

"There's no other word to describe you."

The sincerity in his tone kept me from snorting again.

"Do you say that to every woman Elite contracts you to fuck?" I hadn't meant for the words to come out so blunt, but I'd never been known to have a lot of tact.

His brow furrowed for a split second before smoothing out. "No. I don't. And"—he climbed up over my body on his hands and knees—"you've got nothing to feel insecure about. You're the kind of woman a man could get lost in. Your beautiful eyes. Those tits, a juicy sheath for my aching cock, and long legs I can't wait to have wrapped around my waist."

Already primed and ready to rock, I grabbed ahold of his shoulders and tried to pull him down against me.

"Patience." He chuckled and placed his palm between my breasts, pressing me flat.

With a huff, I lay there as told, and he rewarded me with his lips against mine, allowing me to taste his sinful, luscious mouth again. Hops and underlying sweetness of something I couldn't name laced his breath.

I moaned against his lazy, exploring tongue. Shivers rippled through me, pebbling my skin with goose bumps as his lips trailed along my jaw down to the hollow of my throat.

He finally lowered himself, settling on his elbows and filling his hands with my breasts, lifting them close together. "I've never seen such perfect nipples."

I breathed in, ready to snort, but he closed his mouth over one hardened bud, and I groaned instead, my hips moving against him as my ankles locked around his back.

I'd always had super-sensitive nipples, but no man had ever taken me to the edge of climax from suckling and nipping on them.

Jarod, though...

God. I gasped and arched as he bit down, sharp teeth sending a stinging ache through my chest. "Harder."

He pinched both nipples, feathering kisses down my sternum. "You like a little pain, sweet girl?"

"Mmm." I guessed so.

He pressed both breasts pressed together and ran his tongue across my nipples. "Ever play with clamps?"

I shook my head and pushed his head back to my aching nubs.

He bit down on both at the same time.

"Oh, fuck!" Pain zinged through my flesh, arching my back again and sizzling into sheer need as the tingles raced to my clit. "I'm going to come." I gasped and ground my pelvis against his hard stomach.

He released my breasts and slid lower, open-mouthed, wet kisses leaving a trail of dampness along my rib cage and navel.

I whined a complaint, but the anticipation of where his talented mouth approached kept me from begging him to search that black bag for some clamps.

Too damn slowly, he maneuvered lower, coming to a rest between my thighs.

"Pure heaven," he murmured against my clit.

I lifted my hips, and he gathered my ass in his hands, his tongue sliding over my tight, throbbing nub and down through the center of my swelled lips. He licked and lapped, but my core replenished every drop of arousal he swallowed while groaning his appreciation of how I tasted on his tongue.

Arms overhead and eyes clenched shut, I panted, chest heaving as he took his good old damn time driving me insane. All that existed in that moment was desire bubbling up inside me and his mouth tempting me to the edge. No man had turned me on like Jarod. No single date had ever coursed such intense longing for release in my core. No one had tempted me to even think about having them hang around a little longer than was safe.

Jarod slid two fingers deep inside me, stealing my thoughts.

I moaned, biting the inside of my lip as he flicked my clit with his tongue. "Oh, God," I groaned, my hips writhing for him to move. *Search out my G. Make me come.*

He pulled out and pressed forward again.

"Jarod," I whimpered his name, my voice barely audible from the tingles sweeping through my body, settling between my thighs.

"That's right." He flicked my clit again, his fingers torturous in their slow fucking of my pussy. "I want you to come harder than you ever have, Christine," he whispered against my throbbing nub and curled his fingers.

Magical. Fucking. Spot.

My back bowed off the bed, my breath catching—but he stopped.

"Goddamnit, Jarod!" I lifted my hips, chasing his mouth and gasping.

He grinned at me from between my thighs, my juices coating his lips.

"You said you want me to come. Shove those damn fingers back inside me!"

The asshole pinched the inside of my thigh.

"Fuck." My head fell back again as the pain zinged straight to my clit.

"I do," he murmured, kissing where he'd hurt me. "Eventually."

"Fucker."

Jarod chuckled and licked me from asshole to clit,

sliding his fingers deep inside of me again. Curses spewed from my lips as he bit down on my nub with just enough pressure to make my pussy clench.

He took up a pattern of lick, nibble, curl of the fingers, and retreat.

I became a sweating, panting mess, cursing him for teasing me. But I didn't beg for his dick. The anticipation was too sweet. Too achingly delicious.

Jarod groaned between my thighs, and I lifted my head to meet his gaze.

"You're killing me, Christine. I want to be buried deep inside of you. Ask me to fuck you already. Please, woman."

Who could say no to such an ardent request? Besides, the man knew how to use that rigid shaft he'd been blessed with. The man was definitely worth crossing lines for.

I could give in this once.

"Fuck me, Jarod."

Chapter 10

Jarod

Thank Christ, because I was about ready to blow my load onto her sheets. I crawled up her body, and a breath before I slid deep inside her, I remembered the condom I'd tossed on the nightstand after laying her on the bed.

She was so fucking responsive, hotly vocal, and her liking the slightest bit of pain...

My hands shook while tearing open the wrapper. Couldn't get into her fast enough.

"Hurry," she whispered, her gaze on my hard-as-a-rock, leaking cock.

Fuck, did I lust to shove in and fuck us both into a coma, but she wanted slow. And she hadn't yet begged in the way I needed to hear her.

I settled between her thighs, and she clamped her legs around my waist.

"Goddamn," I groaned, pressing into her soaked sheath until she clenched every inch I had to offer. Holding still, I rested my forehead against hers. Didn't move. Didn't want to blow too early. Fucking woman swiped away my self-control like a wave against the shifting sand. "So damn good." I gyrated my hips, rubbing against her clit.

"Yes," Christine hissed and arched, her head tilting back in offering.

I ignored the need in my cock and slowly rocked in and out of her body, tasting her neck. Sliding my tongue along her collarbone. Sucking on her ear until she shivered beneath me.

Her nails scratched down my back, grounding me and giving me a sweet sting to focus on rather than the need to lose control and attempt to split her lush body in half.

Sweat beaded on my brow, but I continued in my slow, torturous thrusts. Wet suction sounds blended with our moans and groans as I pulled out, pressed in deep, and ground my hips against her.

Yes, she'd asked me to fuck her, but I needed more.

Without thought, I captured her mouth. Full-on, open-mouthed kissing, tongues fucking with the same slow rhythm of our bodies. I tangled my fingers in her hair, holding her head as her arms and legs grasped at my body as though needing to keep me close.

A spark of unease rippled down my spine at the intimacy—the energy—rippling between us, but I couldn't bring myself to stop kissing her soft lips.

While Elite's only strict policy focused on safe words for BDSM play and satisfying clients, I usually stayed away from leisurely kissing while fucking. Tasting a woman's mouth tended to bring on too many emotions, the danger of creating a bond I had no desire for.

But I'd been drawn in from the onset. First eye contact. The first scent of her, the warmth of her skin on mine—

Christine whimpered, her hips wiggling as though she approached the point of desperation and begging. I forced my lips off hers to clear my head, my focus riveting on what I'd promised, what I wanted from her. I palmed the side of her large breast and brought the hard nipple to my mouth.

Her back arched and fingernails dug into my scalp as I nibbled.

"Mmm," she moaned.

A few more laves in sync with my rotating hips, and I thrust hard, biting down on her nipple at the same time.

"Oh, fuck!"

I did it again, my gaze on her face, watching how the slight sting of pain aroused her even more. Her eyes clenched shut, head tipped back, mouth slightly open as she emitted that telltale whine.

Propped on an elbow, my fingers still grasping the soft flesh of her breast, I snaked my other hand between us. I rubbed my thumb along her protruding clit, and she writhed beneath me.

"More." She gasped, lifting her hips against my hand with each slow, full thrust of my cock. "Harder," she whined again as I continued my slow torture.

Biting back a grin, I sucked her nipple deep into my mouth, my thumb flicking and stopping before she crested.

"Goddamnit, Jarod!" Christine slapped my shoulder. "Quit being a fucking tease and give it to me already!"

Grinning, I upped my pace, wishing like hell I had her soaked pussy clutching at my cock with nothing between us. Her heat squeezing me tight. I bit and pinched one last time before straightening so our foreheads rested against each other's again.

Submitting to the need to fuck like an animal, I gently

wrapped my hand around her neck, changed the angle of my hips, and let loose, hard and fast, my pubic bone bruising against hers with every thrust.

Her body convulsed, and her fingernails dug deeper, but I ignored the pain and soaked in the feel of her clutching at me.

"Choke me," she gasped, eyes already glazing over, her body on the verge of explosion.

I tightened my grip.

"Jarod!" She shrieked, her dripping sheath like a vise grip on my cock.

Hissing through my clenched jaw, I rode her orgasm out until she whimpered, shuddering beneath me.

"One more, sweet girl," I rasped and reached for her clit again.

"Oh, shit," she breathed, blinking up at me, pupils blown and lips parted.

Drown, my mind whispered, tempting me to let loose in every aspect, to hand over my heart on a fucking platter.

Christine gave in with a loud groan, her clutching inner walls pulling on me.

I released control over my body only, and my climax readied by tingling up through my legs into my tight-as-hell balls. Spunk erupted from my shaft, filling the condom.

Jesus Christ… Christine…

I swallowed hard, refusing to call out her name, to show vulnerability I couldn't spare. Cursing instead, I jolted with an aftershock, resting my body fully against hers. Forehead to forehead, both heaving for breath, we inhaled the other's exhales.

The scent of cum and sweet honeysuckle filled my nose, the rapid beat of her heart in time with mine as though wrapped around one another, dismissing the skin and bone separating them. Too sated at that moment to care, I allowed the moment to linger, soaking in the sense of rightness, the warmth of being held in her arms.

Our eyes opened at the same time, and I lifted my head slightly to drink her in.

Her green eyes, sated and hazed by passion, reached through whatever barriers I thought I'd held against emotion. A fucking hammer slammed me in the sternum, ripping a grunt from my lungs.

What. The. Fuck.

My eyebrows furrowed, and her gaze cleared, became guarded.

An invisible shield slammed into place—on both our parts.

She smiled, but the upturned lips appeared forced. "I need another beer."

I rolled off her without a word, hand on my chest, focused on the ceiling while trying to ease the strange ache beneath my palm. What the fuck *had* happened? And why did her shutting me out hurt even though I'd done the exact same thing to her?

My attention roamed to her backside as she padded across the floor and bent to pick up her clothing, her round ass and thighs making my mouth water. I still had enough gas left in my tank to take her for another ride even though I'd busted a nut like I hadn't done in a long-ass time.

I had almost groaned her name while blowing my load— something I'd never done with *any* woman, had never even been tempted to do. I scratched my fingers along my chest, baffled. Thoroughly concerned and yet determined to stride through until the end, I lay there for a few moments longer.

Three times, I'd promised Elite's client.

Christine wanted impersonal?

I would give her one last fuck she would never forget, without a single emotion to confuse either of us. Hell, it was what I got paid for, what Micah trusted me to do.

And I aimed to please regardless of the unease slithering down my spine.

Chapter 11

Christine

After tossing my dirty clothes in the hamper, I grabbed a long Pats T-shirt from a drawer and tugged it on—all without glancing at my bed and the beautiful slab of man-beef that had just rocked my world. I needed to straighten my head out.

He's an escort. He gets paid to fuck like that—the shared breaths, emotional gazes bullshit. He's not the guy I need to fall for.

I grabbed a beer from the fridge and gulped the cold bitterness until the lack of oxygen released my lips from the bottle's rim. Mind turning to my growling stomach, I rifled through my near-empty cabinets.

The shuffling of feet announced Jarod's arrival behind me.

"I'm starved," I said without turning, and I pulled open the fridge again. "You hungry?"

"Food sounds good."

God, the timbre of his low voice...

"I've got bunny greens, leftover rotisserie chicken..." Squeezing my thighs together, I yanked open the freezer, a grin finally relaxing me. "Frozen waffles and Canadian bacon. Score."

"Bacon makes everything better."

I grabbed a frying pan, trying like hell to forget the presence of male perfection seeming to steal the air from my small kitchen.

"Can I do anything to help?" he asked.

As if I could survive being all domestic and shit with the man. I reconsidered how to best cook our food to get onto the next order of events for our night together. "Pretty sure I can toast frozen waffles and nuke some bacon." I motioned to the table before putting the frying pan back where I'd found it. "Have a seat."

Three slices each into the microwave finished off the pack, and I moved into the living room to click on the TV for distraction. "Want a beer?" I asked, striding into the kitchen, still without looking at him.

"Water's good."

"Ice?"

"No, thanks."

I flipped the switch on my faucet to turn on the filter and filled a glass, my belly squirming around like a kid who'd done something wrong and was waiting to be found out.

"Thank you," he murmured as I sat his drink on the table in front of him without making eye contact. "You okay?"

Nope. No way. You've ruined me.

"Mmm," I hummed an affirmative regardless of my churning insides and popped two waffles into my toaster. He stayed quiet behind me as I pulled the butter and syrup from the fridge. Since I hadn't kicked him out like all the other guys—and had at least one last fuck with my paid escort before night's end—I forced myself to look at him.

The sight of Jarod stole my breath.

His mussed dark hair was a riotous mess because of my hands. Those dark, mysterious eyes seemed to see straight down to the deepest parts of me. A shirtless chest showed off ripped muscles...

My tongue wanted a taste. Lips tingled as his lifted in a slow smirk.

I forced a smile in return even as the hairs on my nape rose to attention. Shit inside my head and the atmosphere around us needed to be put back to cold reality. The toaster dinged, and I turned away again to busy myself popping in two more.

"Elite's like the perfect job," I said, cringing as I forced myself to speak. "Get paid to fuck with no strings attached. Any chance you could put in a good word for me? I could use a second income."

Jarod cleared his throat as I turned with our plates, my breath held. A furrow lined his forehead, and he wouldn't meet my gaze. "It helps to pay the bills."

I set his plate in front of him. "But?" I asked, sliding onto the chair across from him.

"No buts."

"Then why the frown?" I poured syrup over my waffles and slid the bottle across the table to him as though unfazed by his close proximity that had my nerves on edge.

Fists clenched on the table beside his plate, he lifted his gaze to my face.

My squirming insides tumbled head over heels at his inquisitive stare. "What?" I asked before shoving a piece of bacon in my mouth to give myself something to do.

He pursed his lips and shook his head. "Nothing."

I focused on my food and tried not to fidget until he finally picked up the syrup. We ate in tense silence that strangely wasn't uncomfortable.

"Got a couple more in the box if you're still hungry," I said.

"No, I'm good."

Sports talk droned in the background on the TV, giving me something to think about rather than the tension between us.

"Can I ask you a personal question?" he asked, pushing his cleaned plate away.

I gripped my beer and lifted it toward my lips. "Sure."

"Why are you still single?"

Snorting around my mouthful of beer, I set the bottle back on the table. I forked my last bite of bacon and shoved it into my mouth. "I get bored too easily," I spoke around the food.

"Bored, huh?"

"Yep."

"If that's the case, the men you've been with obviously don't know what they're doing."

I lifted a brow and met his gaze. "Unlike you?"

He grinned, startling butterflies to life in my chest. "I don't hear too many complaints."

I smirked but refused to stroke his ego by stating I could imagine he didn't.

"It's all about reading your woman. Figuring out her likes and dislikes. Deepest desires and fantasies."

My brow pulled down for a second. "I've never kept a guy around long enough to get into the deep stuff."

"Why not?"

"They didn't interest me or were boring as hell." I

shrugged. "I've never had a chance to put myself out there like that." Not that I would if even if given the chance.

"Can't make a connection if you don't allow yourself to be vulnerable."

I eyed him for a few seconds before replying. "I don't have walls up if that's what you mean."

Jarod leaned back in the chair, tipping onto its back legs while eyeing me as though wanting to call me out on my bullshit. "Everyone has walls of some sort, and most can be crumbled in the right circumstances."

"Reid and Jessie," I stated.

He nodded.

"It was worth my bonus," I murmured, thinking about the two of them, the happiness I saw on my friend's face every day at work.

"Your bonus?"

I shrugged. "I used it to give Jessie that date with him." I smirked across the table at Jarod. "Originally, I'd planned to spoil myself by booking an evening with you because you're hella hot, but she needed a night of freedom more than I did your dick. I'd say it all worked out the way it was meant to."

He once more studied my face with an intensity that made me antsy. "That was a very unselfish thing to do."

"Meh." I brushed off his words of praise. "She's one of my best friends and never got to experience freedom or a good time thanks to her ex. A person has to *live*. Do all the things so there are no regrets. You could be in the basement switching your laundry and get trapped by fire—" I cut off and swallowed hard before forcing a fake-as-shit smile.

"Don't."

"Don't what?" I managed, still trying for brightness I did not feel.

"That was too specific, and the hurt in your eyes is

making my chest ache." Dark orbs filled with empathy peered at me, further tightening my throat.

Only a handful of people knew what had happened to my mom, but for some reason, I found myself wanting him to understand why I chose to live the way I did when seconds earlier I'd been locked up like a clam. Perhaps it was the softness in Jarod's eyes. Maybe it had been the way he peered into my soul in those moments after we'd climaxed together. We had been bound up in an emotional connection I didn't know how to name.

"My dad and I went to see the Sox," I whispered, hating how weak I sounded and yet determined to explain why my heart would never be available for the taking. "Mom had tried calling Dad, but of course, neither of us heard his cell ring. We were leaving Fenway when he checked his messages. She had called to say goodbye."

"Oh, fuck," he breathed the words, easily putting two and two together. Jarod reached over the table and grabbed hold of my hand.

His strong fingers laced through mine, offering comfort. Neither of us spoke, and I swallowed down threatening tears.

"We have to live every day, every moment, as though it's our last," I finally stated quietly.

Jarod nodded, his thumb rubbing over the back of my hand in a too-sweet gesture that restarted my unease from earlier.

"God, enough of this deep shit already," I stated with a forced laugh while pulling from his hold and sitting back in my chair.

He seemed to understand my need for space and only hesitated a second before crossing his arms on the table and leaning forward, his eyes taking on a flirty glint.

My blood heated instantly, regardless of the heaviness we'd just escaped.

"I'm a near-stranger, hired for the night to fulfill your sexual fantasies. So..." His slow smirk twinged arousal between my thighs. "What's your number one?"

My face heated as warmth rushed through my body.

"Oh, this is going to be good." He full-on grinned. "Come on. Spill the truth that's making your pupils swell."

Considering what I'd told him about Mom, there was no point in holding back. "I want to be watched."

One of Jarod's eyebrows rose. "You're an exhibitionist?"

Face even hotter, I shrugged. "Tonight when you made me come on the dance floor is the closest I've been to being on display before, but I've dreamed about it."

"Having someone watch you masturbate, or a crowd getting off on a man making you come until you black out?"

"Not a bunch of people." I shifted on my seat, my core clenching at emptiness. "Just one man in a dark corner, like a peeking Tom all secretive and shit."

"Well, damn. Had I known sooner, I could have brought someone along to fulfill that one."

My throat went dry in a flash. "That would have been hot. One professional escort fucking me, another watching us..." A shudder rippled down through me as a huff of laughter flitted past my lips. "You'd ruin me for life for *sure*."

Jarod peered at me until I shifted again, realizing I'd let the truth of what he did to me slip.

"What?" I asked, sounding way too breathless and needy.

"I *could* make a call."

A thrill shot through me, pulsing my core even though I was one last round away from being done. "Seriously?"

"Dead. One of Elite's newest hires also works as a Dom over at Chantelle's and would probably be into that. He lives not too far from here too."

So that rumor about a BDSM club was real.

"What if he's on the clock?"

"What if he's not?" Jarod shot back, his eyes full of mischief.

The tip of my tongue found my top lip. "I can't afford to pay another escort."

Jarod's gaze roamed down my neck, to my pebbled nipples pressing against my T-shirt. "My treat."

Not that I really cared, but I glanced at the clock. I'd really rather have had the situation set up in advance and made to look like a clandestine meeting that someone just happened to stumble upon.

"Or we could save it for next time," he murmured.

My gaze jerked back to Jarod. God, did I want to ask him what he'd meant, but I *so* wasn't going there. "Tell me one of your fantasies," I said instead.

His focus dipped low to my pebbled nipples again. "The second I first laid eyes on you moving at the club, I wanted to be buried balls deep inside of your ass."

My pussy clenched, releasing enough moisture to soak through my shirt beneath me and leave a wet spot on my chair when I stood.

"Have you had anal sex before?" he asked before I could respond.

"Yes."

"Did you like it?"

"It was too...loving." I cringed at the memory of honey-coated words and gentle nudges up my backside. "If you're going to fuck my ass, fuck it. Don't make love to it."

Jarod's gaze burned into me. "I'm up for round three if you are."

And be further wrecked for all future hookups?

I nodded and ignored the blaring alarms going off in my head. "Fuck yeah."

Chapter 12

Jarod

I'd lied. My dick was *way* more than up for another go at Christine's body and had been except for that brief moment when she'd told me about her mom. Pushing the memory of the unfinished story from my mind, I focused on the gorgeous woman tempting me to change almost everything about my existence.

"What?" she asked, her breathless tone along with the tight nipples poking at her T-shirt promising me a wet pussy.

I guessed I'd hesitated a few seconds too long after offering to be of service. Standing, I rounded the table and held out a hand in invitation.

Christine slid her palm against mine, and I pulled her to her feet. Rather than going for her lips, I spun her body and tugged her close against my chest as I'd done at the dance club. One arm wrapped around her waist, I released her hand and moved her hair off to the side, baring her pale neck.

My dick bucked, my mouth drooling to suckle and bruise her up for the world to see.

Nope.

Still, I clamped onto her soft skin, teeth nibbling, but not hard enough to leave a mark like the hickey I'd gifted her breast where no one would notice.

She went boneless, sagging against me in sweet surrender that fueled the fire in my blood.

Shuffling her forward to the island, I took us both where I wanted to go. The countertop pressed against her hips, and I pushed her torso down, chest flat against the granite. Forget the gentleness of our earlier messing around on her bed. She'd all but asked for my dick hard and deep up her ass with a lack of emotions. I couldn't think of a more perfect way to end the evening and stop whatever had gone down before our late-night snack.

I kicked her feet apart and palmed her ass, honeysuckle and creamy pussy overriding the savory smell of bacon lingering in the air.

"You like it rough?" I whispered against her ear and shoved two fingers deep inside of her soaked sheath.

She whimpered as though unable to form words, squirming in my hold.

Two thrusts, and I pulled my fingers free, lifting them to my mouth. I inhaled deeply, drawing the musky scent of her into my lungs.

"You smell so damn good." I sucked her tangy sweetness of my fingers. "Taste even better."

Christine cursed under her breath, shifting beneath my other palm on her lower back.

"Don't move." Grinding against her ass, I grabbed the black bag off the other end of the island and pulled it toward me.

Christine panted but stayed put like I'd commanded while I rifled through the goodies supplied by Elite.

I sat a vibrating dildo and condom beside her hip but kept the bottle of lube in hand, snapping open the cap to drip it down her crack.

Her rosebud clenched as the clear liquid slid over its puckered skin.

Fuck, I couldn't wait to see her hole wink at me when I pulled my spent dick out. Too fucking bad my spunk would get caught in the condom rather than dribble free.

Teeth gritted, I sheathed myself, eyeing her tight hole and the glistening pussy beneath. She wanted it rough, but no way in fuck would I shove in without prepping her a bit first. Grasping her cheeks, I spread them wide and ran the back of my dick up through her crack, smearing the lube.

Christine arched her back and moaned like a cat in heat.

I took her up on her offering but with a single finger rather than the fat head of my cock.

She hissed as I probed with a fingertip.

"Been a while?"

"Yeah."

I slid in, cursing at her silken heat sucking on my finger. "Can't wait to be inside your tight ass."

She wiggled her backside, and I removed my touch to get more lube, working it inside her with a second finger, scissoring to stretch her out. Three would have been a good idea, but she wanted to feel it.

I pulled out of her hole, lubed up my rigid dick, and wiped my fingers off on her bunched T-shirt. Wrapping my hand in her hair, I tugged harshly, yanking her upright against my chest.

"I'm going to fuck your ass, Christine." I bit down on her earlobe and reached around to run two fingers along either side of her clit. "If it's too much, tell me to stop, and I will."

She moaned and arched.

Dipping into her pussy, my fingers found slick wetness to smear up over her hard nub. I pinched hard, sliding my dick up through her crack. "Okay?" I pushed for acknowledgment of what I'd promised. "No games right now. No means no, stop ceases all interaction, understand?"

"Yes." She half-gasped the word, her panted exhales like an electrical charge to my already tensed body.

I pushed her down onto the island and yanked both of her arms behind her back, gathering her wrists in one hand. "Breathe out and relax, sweet girl," I murmured, gripping my dick at the base and guiding my throbbing tip to her puckered hole.

She went pliant—and I shoved forward, almost filling her up with one thrust.

"Fuck!" She shrieked and jerked forward, but I grabbed her hip, holding her still as she breathed through the stinging pain she must be feeling.

When she didn't ask for me to back out or tell me it was too much, I pulled out to the tip and slammed back in, balls deep just like I'd fantasized about.

"Ah, fuck," I groaned as Christine shuddered beneath me. "So. Fucking. Tight." I growled the words in time with three deep-seated thrusts.

"Harder," she whispered as I drove forward again with a grunt, burying inside her heat.

Fighting against the throb in my balls, I released my grasp on her hip and grabbed the vibrator, snaking it between the island and her pelvis.

The vibrator burst into action against her clit as I backed away and shoved deep inside her once more.

"Oh, God." Her ass lifted higher with each of my violent thrusts until she stood on my tiptoes, both of our animal-like grunts filling my ears. "I'm going to come. Holy... Jarod!" An orgasm tore through her, body convulsing as I continued to slam into her over and over, my balls slapping against her soaked pussy.

"That's right, sweet girl," I ground out, pressing the vibrator harder against her clit. "Give it to me."

Christine writhed beneath me, another whine building in her chest as I stabbed into her ass in a relentless drive to wreck her for any other man.

I slid the vibrator down against her lower lips and leaned over her back. "One more," I demanded against her ear, angling the vibrator to slide it deep into her pussy.

A shriek passed her lips, and she arched off the island, gifting me her hardest climax yet.

My teeth clamped down on her shoulder without thought as my dick bucked inside her ass, the vibrations of the toy a membrane of skin away from my dick, spinning my head.

Hips stuttering, my balls released, every spurt into the condom causing my entire body to spasm, tightening my abs.

"Fuuuuck," I drawled out the curse, shivering with the final release of cum from my sac.

My muscles slackened as I slid the toy from her pussy and tossed it onto the island. I sagged against Christine, fighting to catch my breath. She panted beneath me, spent as fuck. A smile curved her lips in profile from where she rested her cheek against the granite.

An ache took up residence in my chest again, and hissing, I straightened rather than burying my face in her neck and loving on her soft skin until my limp dick slid free from her tight ass. One last gift to myself...

I grasped her cheeks and slowly backed out, a shudder ripping through me as her slackened hole winked up at me like I'd wanted to see.

Cursing the load trapped inside the condom, I squeezed her flesh and popped a swat on her backside, jiggling the rounded peach calling out for my teeth. "Any complaints?" I asked, going for a light tone and not sure I'd managed it.

She huffed a laugh, sounding carefree and not nearly as fucked up inside as I was. "Not a single one."

Another client well and truly satisfied.

So why didn't I feel the sense of pride I usually did while heading to the bathroom to clean up?

Chapter 13

Christine

Intent on the coffeepot, I meandered past my kitchen island, memories from the night before heating my blood and twinging me between my sore thighs.

"So." Jess's barely-held excitement came through loud and clear over my cell as I tried to push images of Jarod with his eyes closed and head tipped back while unloading in my ass from my mind.

I failed. Miserably. I also didn't know how to give Jessie what she had called for.

"Come on. Spill already. How'd it go?"

"How long have you been awake, wanting to call me?" I asked while reaching for the coffeepot, trying to figure out a way to fulfill her desire and protect myself. "An hour?"

"Well?" she pushed with a huff rather than answering me.

"It was fan-fucking-tastic with a capital F," I purred the half-lie, needing to stick to my usual cold self. Jarod had more than risen above my expectations—but he'd also left a train wreck in the wake of his presence.

Jessie laughed in my ear, but I couldn't find an ounce of

jollity to join in her excitement over hearing memories I'd rather forget.

"Could the poor man even walk when you finally finished with him?"

Neither of us had been steady on our feet, but I had sent him packing regardless of how much I'd longed to beg him to spend the rest of the night. I didn't doubt we would have ended up back in my bed, snuggling and cuddling. Probably pillow talking clear into the early morning hours where we could have fucked one last time before eight rolled around. Doing so would have ensured I fell even harder than I'd ever imagined possible.

Heaviness hovered over my chest, my mood as dim as the gray sky out my kitchen window. Pouring my second cup of coffee, I attempted to escape the sense of loss hanging over my mind. "He walked out without argument," I stated the truth, taking care to keep the disappointment from my tone. *Without a backward glance either.* Eyes stinging, I cleared my throat, needing to keep to hard facts Jessie would enjoy hearing about. "He came three times—six or so for me. I lost count."

"Oh, shit." Jessie snickered.

"Yep. Best lay in..." My eyebrows scrunched as I considered and put the pot back. "My life, really."

"Double shit." Her tone suggested she knew exactly what had gone down between Jarod and me the night before. Hell, she'd experienced the same with Reid. A connection too powerful to ignore.

A shiver slid down my spine, and I lifted my mug for a sip, acting like everything was normal when it was far from it.

"Talk to me, Christine," Jessie said, and I exhaled long and loudly.

"He's scary," I admitted before blowing the steam rising from the black liquid that couldn't make everything better like I always claimed coffee could do. "I could totally fall for him." Or maybe I already had? Was that possible after a three-ring circus of fucking ourselves silly? It was probably just my sated hormones climbing aboard the *more* train.

"Oh boy," Jessie murmured.

I swallowed the hot, black brew while closing my eyes and allowing myself to relive the experience of Jarod for a moment. "He made me feel things. A stir of emotion I haven't experienced before. His stare suggested he sensed that connection as well." Pursing my lips, I shook my head, reminding myself of the danger of falling for a man who got paid to make women swoon. "He's an escort and probably stares that way at every client. It's part of fulfilling his job."

"Bullshit," Jessie countered, biting out the word. "Reid gave off those vibes on our first date too, and look where we ended up."

"Jarod is the kind of guy who would hold my attention for quite a while if I gave him a chance." My eyelids popped open against the image of the two of us together again flitting through my mind—before being abruptly cut off by the flames licking around us, the shadow of doom and the promise of heartache.

It was time to get shit back in order inside my head and pick back up the Christine persona I would only allow men to see. "I would grow bored eventually though and end up breaking his heart like all the rest."

"Maybe not," Jessie suggested, but I couldn't begin to go along with her thoughts.

The desire that had stirred up inside me the night before while Jarod had slowly and thoroughly made love to me...

Not love.

I shook my head, refusing the word. He'd simply given me what I'd asked for. "He's one hell of an escort and a scary son of a bitch," I murmured.

"So when are you seeing him again?" My friend asked, bringing to mind to the "next time" Jarod had suggested when I'd told him about my exhibition fantasy.

"He's too expensive to book on a regular schedule." Damn dangerous as well.

"So other than the sex, how was your night?"

"We hardly spoke at all in the beginning, but I found out the two most important things. He loves beer and sports."

Jessie laughed. "You should start saving your pennies or find a way to get him in your bed without exchanging money because from what I know about Jarod from you and Reid, the two of you are a match made in heaven."

I considered the twinge in my chest and gripped my coffee mug tighter while heading to the living room. "I'm not fool enough to even consider that fantasy." I also had a strong sense of self-preservation thanks to the tragic event I'd for some reason told Jarod about. He had been so empathetic, figuring out the truth about my mom without my having to spell shit out clearly in black and white.

"Do you think he likes you back?" she asked.

The memory of the emotion in his dark eyes as he came after the slow torture flitted through my brain and filled me with the same wariness as it had the night before. I didn't care how good of an actor Jarod had to be to work for Elite. He'd felt it. He'd also shut that shit down as quickly and as firmly as I had. "Yeah. I do," I finally admitted out loud.

"So what's the problem?"

"I don't do relationships, Jessie," I firmly reminded her while sitting on my couch and tucking my legs beneath me.

"Maybe you ought to give it a try."

"And break another heart?" I scoffed rather than speaking the truth that even *she* didn't know about my mom and how I feared such deep sorrow. So why the hell had I opened up like that with a paid escort I'd only just met? I grabbed the clicker and turned on the TV, needing distraction and a sense of normalcy I'd lost overnight. "I'll keep to the casual fuck when I need some action and my single, quiet life, thank you very much."

The flippant statement didn't soothe or lessen the heaviness in my chest. I'd expected moving on from the fuck of a lifetime would be difficult, but damn. Hopefully, every passing day would lessen the rich memories of Jarod's touch, the taste of his tongue, and the feel of him sliding deep inside me as though seeking out a place to make his own.

A shudder wracked my body, and I barely managed to keep from spilling my coffee on my lap.

"Are you going to watch the Pats this afternoon?" Jessie asked, knowing my stubbornness all too well and taking me at my feigned declaration.

I chuckled, glad for the change of conversation. "Season tickets thanks to Uncle Bradley. Dad and I plan on being at every game this year, same as always."

"You're lucky to have a dad—and to have so much in common with him." Jessie's sighed words hit me hard but for dual reasons.

Compassion over the lack of a father figure in her life but also an almost...premonition?

I had always protected myself to never be dealt the blow Dad had experienced at Mom's death.

And I sure as hell did *not* want to go through the same because I wasn't nearly as strong as my father. Falling for Jarod and giving in to the lust, the yearning for that next time would bring about a heartache I wouldn't be able to survive.

Chapter 14

Jarod

I didn't sleep worth a shit. All I could think about was Christine—her sweet curves, green, smiling eyes, and her love of the things I enjoyed the most. Her scent had remained in my nose for hours after I'd crawled into bed, denying my ability to mentally shut down and rest my body. She was like the purest drug and had hit my blood with a rush beyond anything I'd ever felt before, keeping me awake long into the early morning hours.

At least I had other shit to keep me busy after I'd dragged my weary ass out of bed. As with every Sunday, Micah, his brother Sean, and Cooney, Elite's newest hire, would hang out at my condo for the day's football games. Blake and Reid used to come over too, but I couldn't be mad at the women who'd stolen their hearts. Had I fallen as hard as they had, I probably would be caught up in the same way, my friends taking a back seat to more important things in life.

I understood after having met Christine and feeling that connection between us as strong as an electrical current hell-bent on jumpstarting a heart I claimed to not have.

And that fact scared the shit out of me.

She enamored me. Stole into my brain with pure witchery. Sank claws into my chest as though needing purchase—a solid foundation on which to build the rest of her life. Someone to care for her. To hold her.

But I had nothing to offer and told myself I didn't want to even if I did have space in my soul.

I adjusted myself through my jeans before pulling the wings off the grill out on my enclosed back patio. Forgetting about Christine wouldn't come easily regardless of the Patriot's anticipated game with Pittsburgh. I'd spent the previous couple of hours cleaning up my place and getting all our usual tailgating food ready for the guys. Nacho dip sat in the oven, a couple six packs cooled in my fridge. They would bring a few other snacks as well, and we would all end up buzzed and feeling stuffed full as turkeys on Thanksgiving Day.

My doorbell rang, and I let myself back through the screen slider into my kitchen, set the bowl of wings on the counter, and made my way through the hallway into my foyer. Micah and his brother Sean stood on the stoop.

"What's up?" I asked, stepping out of the way to let them in.

Micah clasped my hand, his other arm bearing a grocery bag. "Jarod."

I ruffled Sean's dirty blond hair like I always did, turning his grin into a scowl. "Hey, kid."

"Not a fucking kid," he grumbled, sidestepping to escape me.

Snickering, I went to shut the door but noted Daniel Cooney pulling in front of my condo in his Cherokee.

I waited for him as Micah and Sean made for the kitchen to unload their food.

Cooney glanced around the neighborhood as he climbed from his vehicle, dark eyes cataloging everything in the vicinity as he did every time he showed up somewhere. The man was careful. Calculating. Seemed the type to have at your back whenever shit hit the fan. And at 6'5" and ripped as fuck, he promised to be one hell of an adversary.

He took a crockpot out of the back of his car, leaving the door open.

"What's in there?" I asked as he drew near, red hair mussed to hell as usual but his short beard meticulously trimmed.

"Homemade meatballs."

"Fuck yeah." I took the pot as he held it out to me.

"Got rolls too—be right back." He turned and strode toward the car, but I waited for him rather than head to the kitchen.

Once Cooney locked up and headed my way, I let him in on what had gone down the evening before.

"Almost called you last night," I said, kicking my front door shut behind his big ass as he stepped past me, two bags in his meaty paws.

"For?" He grunted the word, moving back through the hallway.

"The client I was with has an exhibitionist fantasy. Figured you're into all that other kinky shit so you'd be up for it."

"Other kinky shit?" he questioned.

"BDSM—ropes and such."

He grunted, but I couldn't make heads or tails of the noise.

"It's rumored you do demonstrations over at Chantelle's," I tacked on.

Cooney shot a glance over at me while sitting his stuff

on the counter, his gaze piercing. "Who'd you hear that from?"

"Micah."

His lips pressed tight.

"So it is true? You like to tie chicks up and whip their asses?"

"Yes and no." In the short time I'd known Cooney, I'd recognized him for the reserved, quiet type he was.

"That's all you're giving me?" I pushed, grinning.

"Yep."

Chuckling, I grabbed a couple of beers out of the fridge and handed him one. We both popped the lids, clinked our bottles together, and took healthy pulls. Smooth, hop-infused coldness slid down my throat, and I made a noise of appreciation.

Rather than pushing, I strode into the living room where Micah and Sean had sprawled on my sectional facing the wide-screen TV anchored into the wall above my gas fireplace.

"How was your date last night?" Micah asked as I settled into my usual seat, a recliner angled on the couch's opposite end from him.

"Hot as fuck. She's also the type of woman I would give up my second job for." I bit my tongue, not having meant to state the truth that had slammed into my brain within moments of catching sight of the fiery redheaded temptress.

"No fucking way, Zimmerman," Micah shot at me, his brow denting into a scowl. "It's bad enough Sullivan bailed on me after meeting Jessie. I still haven't replaced the other half of your tall, dark, and handsome duo."

While Micah had often joined up with me to fulfill client threesome wishes, we were polar opposites. He was a golden boy with blond hair and a shade darker close-clipped beard, impeccably groomed along his jaw like Cooney's.

"Just said she was that type," I grumbled. "Didn't say I had any plans of quitting on you."

Cooney and Micah shared a look as the bigger man dropped onto the cushion closest to me.

"What?" I asked, bottle halfway to my lips, my gaze jumping between the two.

"You're fucked, that's what," Cooney stated as though sure of that fact.

"Don't even fucking say that." Micah glowered at him. "And"—he turned his attention on me— "don't you even fucking *think* that."

I shook my head and tried to focus on the coin toss happening on TV. "I'm not thinking that." *Liar*. I chugged my beer.

Sean snorted. "Definitely fucked."

I had left Christine's a few minutes after taking her ass over the island in her kitchen. Exactly like the first time against her front door, she'd walked away with a sway to her backside as though unfazed by the fact my cock had been buried deep inside of it a minute earlier.

She'd come across as though unmoved by our rough exchange. Impersonal exactly like she'd claimed to want— like I'd silently promised. And fuck that goddamn hammer that had slammed me in the chest again as our gazes had met across the kitchen. Her breath had caught, but she'd quietly thanked me for the evening and told me to leave.

Literally ordered me to get out.

Coldhearted bitch...she lit unquenchable fires inside me. I pinched the bridge of my nose and closed my eyes, missing the kickoff.

"That's right, Davis," Cooney's voice rose, showing a hint of passion. "Stiff arm that fucker."

"Goddamn, what a return," Micah said a second later, which lifted my head off the couch.

The punt return team exited the field, but my mind refused to acknowledge the beginning of the game. Was the memory of Christine going to haunt me all fucking day long?

"Didn't you have a new client Thursday?" I asked Micah, desperate to turn my mind off of Christine.

"I got to wield my favorite cane."

Like Cooney, Micah got off on different forms of kink too. He'd only recently taken on clients of his own after Sean had pushed him to expand Elite's services. Sean had wanted a gay branch, but Micah went the route he understood and enjoyed. Cooney bound the women, and Micah gave them the pain they desired with their pleasure.

"Did she like it?" I asked, fighting off a cringe at the thought of getting whacked with a goddamn cane. I'd heard they hurt like hell.

"Dirty little girl couldn't get enough." Micah adjusted himself, grimacing a bit. "She came four times before I even took her virgin ass. She wanted it deep and hard—and that's exactly what she got. All at once."

Cooney stared Micah down—glared, actually. "She's not going to file a complaint, is she?"

Micah rolled his eyes. "For fuck's sake, Cooney, what do you think I am? A monster? She had a safe word—lollipops of all things. I checked in with her countless times, and yes, she'd begged me to wreck her. Seeing as how she'd paid for my Dom experience, I gave her what she'd wanted."

Lips in a thin line, Cooney nodded and returned his focus back to the TV.

"The best part?" Micah continued, "Right before I'd taken the cane to her ass, she'd asked if her friend from next door could watch."

"Because she has an exhibition kink or her friend's a voyeur?" I asked.

Micah shrugged. "Didn't ask. You know I don't get into the personal shit. I'm just there to fuck and satisfy the pain sluts."

I chuckled, already knowing the answer to my next question. "What if your client wanted to snuggle and chat about her day?"

Micah huffed a snort. "Fuck that shit."

Cooney and I caught one another's eyes. I grinned, and his lips actually quirked. "Pretty sure our employee contracts ensure satisfaction," I said, turning back toward our boss.

"Yeah, well, I'm not an employee, am I?" Micah brushed me off.

"So did that girlfriend end up getting in on the action too?" Sean asked, his lips quirking, blue eyes full of mischief.

"Why the fuck do you care?" Micah punched his little brother's upper arm. "A threesome with two women is the last thing you'd be interested in."

Sean's being gay wasn't a secret, nor was it an issue with their family, same as with the guys we hung out with.

"Give me dick all day long," Sean sang the words. "Better yet, get that male-on-male action for Elite up and running like I've been pushing for, and let me be your most popular escort."

"Mom would kill me," Micah muttered.

I glanced at Cooney who eyed the brothers. "That's not a no," he stated exactly what had come to my mind.

Sean had been after Micah to start offering gay escort services for months, but Micah had flat-out refused. Countless times.

"And why would gay or bi guys pay for an escort when there are hookup apps enough to satisfy any man craving dick?" Micah asked before sucking down his beer.

Again, not his usual response.

"There are lots of straight hookup apps too," Sean said with a shrug, "and yet EE still rakes in the dough."

Micah nodded slowly as though actually listening... considering. But my friend never made up his mind on a whim. He would take hours to consider all aspects, weigh the pros and cons. His biggest pro? Definitely Sean.

I was straight as fuck, but even I could appreciate the kid's good looks. Add in his quirky, sunshiny attitude—never mind his voracious appetite for dick we all heard about constantly—and he would definitely make Elite a killing. He claimed he wasn't a twink even though he was on the shorter side and definitely slender compared to his ripped brother. But he didn't argue about his being a brat and bossy bottom.

All talk of business was set aside as the tension on the gridiron raised to the boiling point.

We sat and watched the close scoring game unfold, a few bullshit calls earning hollered curses from the four of us.

Thoughts of Christine continued to flit through my mind, and I wondered if Cooney had ever been captivated by a client too.

"What have you been up to, Cooney?" I asked, glancing over at the brooding brute during a commercial break. "Did you have a hot date this weekend?"

"Nope. I was at Blushing Cherry when the bomb threat came in Friday night."

"No shit."

"It was awful. The lights flicked on full force, the music cut out, and David told us to get the fuck out. Too bad, too, cuz Lacey was humping that pole like it was her last day on earth."

Micah groaned and grabbed his cock. "Fucking Lacey."

Cooney murmured an agreement.

I laughed under my breath. Both had it bad for the BC's favorite pixie-haired minx of a stripper. It was no secret she enjoyed a good gang bang. Micah and Reid had her once not long after graduating from high school—at the same time. There'd been an exchange of money for the interaction, a joke at the time, but she was the one who'd inspired Micah's enjoyment of threesomes and opened his mind up to the idea of fucking for money. A dozen or so years later, he finally started up the professional escort business that had helped me finish paying for college. The fucker had more money than both Cooney and I would make in our lifetimes with our BAs.

"Fuck!" Micah sat forward on his chair as the Pats's quarterback scrambled from the ten-yard line.

"Move your ass!" Cooney shouted at the same time Sean and I leapt to our feet.

All four of us hollered as he dove, arms and ball outstretched toward the in-zone. The ref's arms went up, and our shouts deafened.

The camera went to the stands to catch a few high-fives and waving arms. An up-close shot of a green-eyed, sexy-as-hell woman with the Pats logo painted on her cheek and beer in her raised hand caught my breath, and I slumped back onto the chair, my breath fucking *gone*.

"She's hot," Cooney said, still standing and eyeing the woman the cameraman lingered on.

Micah stared at the TV and sipped his beer as he sat back down. "I'd fuck her for free."

My stomach knotted at the thought of my boss's dick anywhere near Christine. "That's her."

"Her who?" Cooney asked while settling back onto the couch in my periphery.

The camera zoomed away, and I swallowed, my memory once more burned with the image of those emerald eyes and fiery tresses. "Christine. My date from last night."

"That hot chick on the screen just now?" Micah asked for clarity.

"Yeah." My voice sounded like gravel, and my insides churned like a vat of tumbling pebbles.

"She's a Pats fan? Well, shit." Micah snorted. "No wonder you're lovestruck."

"I'm not lovestruck, fuckwad." I threw one of my crumpled-up napkins at his head.

Cooney hummed under his breath. "Uh huh. Keep lying to yourself, Zimmerman."

I planned to do as my co-worker suggested, but I had a feeling I'd be turning down more of Micah's clients than accepting in the future.

Chapter 15

Christine

Two weeks had passed since I'd sent Jarod packing, and I loathed myself for kicking him out so coldly. I could have clung to him until eight the next morning when the contract between me and Elite had stated our time together officially ended.

Instead, I'd been a self-preserving idiot, and every day that passed made me regret my error.

But had I spent even one more minute in his presence, I would have fallen even harder. It was bad enough that I couldn't rid my mind of the man. The memory of his touch, his kisses, had truly ruined me for anyone else.

For thirteen goddamned days, I went without dick, relying on dildos and vibrators alone to get me off. Not that I'd been truly missing out on much with my random hookups. Jarod had been the first to truly satisfy my cravings when no one before him had even come close.

Wrecked seemed the perfect word to describe what he'd done to me. And I didn't know what to do with that truth.

Chest heavy, I painted on a smile, greeting the next guest to enter the ballroom we had rented for the fundraiser

Uncle Bradley had entrusted to my care. As with any task assigned to me, I'd whipped a plan into place and executed it to perfection, even more easily done in my desire to escape thoughts of the tall drink of water I continued to thirst for.

Uncle Bradley and Dad stood with me while we waited for Auntie Sophie and our little guest of honor. Mary Rose, aka Rosie to me, was an innocent at only seven, but leukemia seemed hell-bent on siphoning the life from her body. Her grandpapa, Uncle Bradley, and grandmama, Auntie Sophie, had taken on the pleasure of raising her when their daughter had proved too mentally unstable to handle the child on her own.

Rosie had never been a burden to her grandparents, and even though the illness and grief they faced had aged both Dad's best friend and his wife in the few months since the little girl's diagnosis, they still loved on her and attempted to give her the world in the time she had left.

And they were desperate to raise awareness and funds to help researchers find a cure so no other child needed to face what she did.

While greeting guests and eventually moving through the crowd of influential people both Dad and Uncle Bradley knew, I thought about Jarod and his experience, or rather, the little he'd shared with me. Unlike Rosie, Jarod had been given the chance to beat cancer's ass and won, even without the loving support of family at his side.

In typical nosey form, I'd checked out Jarod on social media, but he didn't post much. He did, however, make it known to the world he worked at the same hospital Rosie spent most of her time in.

I wondered if they'd met each other—

"Christine," Uncle Bradley called to me from where I

stood speaking with some political prick I could give two shits about since he tended toward a conservative stance on issues I thoroughly aligned myself with. Better treatment of the LGBTQ+ community being the most important to me.

Face hurting from keeping my smile in place, I made my excuses to those I'd been chatting with and turned away, ready for the night to be over when it had only just begun. The heels I'd chosen to wear pinched my toes, the tight, sheath-like dress hugging my pre-menstrual bloat into place. Stifling my inner bitch, I slowly inhaled, imagining exhaling the shit I'd wanted to spew at the state's representative. The asshole felt as though equal rights for all meant fewer rights for him.

He deserved to rot in the hell he believed non-straight people would wind up in someday. How the fuck he ever got into office in the state of Massachusetts, I would never know.

My curved lips rose higher when I caught sight of Uncle Bradley standing with a couple of men I recognized. Nick and Nate from my favorite sports talk show. It wouldn't be the first time we'd conversed thanks to Uncle Bradley working for Pats Nation, and the sight of them promised me a night with less hormonal drama than there had been going on in my head.

Both men had at least a decade on me, were hot enough to warrant a second glance, and unfortunately were happily married to the loves of their lives. I couldn't begin imagining being shacked up for good with a guy who was well-versed in one of my favorite topics.

Jarod knew football—

I cut off the thought since I had hardly anything to base the assumption upon. So what if he'd stated the per-season record of both the Pats and Steelers going into the season? Lots of men had knowledge of those stats, my dad included.

We exchanged pleasantries, and I thanked both Nick and Nate for their shout-out on their show that morning and for sharing information on how others could contribute toward the funds we raised for cancer research.

Minutes later, Uncle Bradley clutched my arm, pulling my focus from our discussion on what New England's defensive coordinator had up his sleeve to stop the Packers the following afternoon. "Darnel Jackson is here."

My head whipped toward the main doors, jaw dropping. "Oh. My. God."

Both Nick and Nate snickered over my fangirling.

The rookie had ended up needing surgery and was out for a couple of weeks, and even though Uncle Bradley had told me Jackson's cousin had leukemia years earlier, I never in a million years expected the man to show up. Along with him came an entourage—including a few front linemen from his team.

Night. Made.

Grinning and feeling giddy—downright high as a kite—I "allowed" myself to be dragged away from my two favorite sports show talk hosts to meet the guests I hadn't known Uncle Bradley had invited.

Talk about a photo fest.

I didn't lower myself to selfies but definitely had Uncle hook me up by being my photographer. He stuffed my cell with images to share once the night ended. Like a kid in a candy store, my gaze flitted from one Patriot to another, salivating to dig into their brains and learn firsthand knowledge from the game on a personal level rather than just what I'd heard on the news and in interviews.

Someone brought beer from the open bar. Clinking

bottles around with a bunch of guys who towered over me—fuckers who actually played football for a living—made that ache on my face from smiling truly worth the energy I'd expended on the event.

The noise level had risen a bit in the ballroom atop the DJ in the room's corner, and I leaned forward to catch what one of the men was saying, my gaze moving past him toward the doors.

Jarod, dressed to kill in a black suit, stood on the threshold, taking in the room.

Butterflies erupted at the same time my core clenched.

Like the athletes, I hadn't expected him of all people to show up, even though the chances were high he at some point had helped care for Rosie.

My gaze flitted to the petite brunette standing beside him, and those butterflies withered and nose-bombed in my belly. The woman was gorgeous. Tiny. Dark to my stark red. She spoke, and Jarod leaned down to better hear her, his hand going to her back.

Were they together? Was she his date? Or was it the other way around?

Fuck.

Swallowing hard, I told myself it didn't matter. Why did I care? The thought he was simply there as hired eye candy for the woman beside him didn't gel since he worked for the hospital where Rosie went for treatment.

They moved into the room together, angling toward a group of people Uncle Bradley had told me worked at the hospital where Rosie went for treatment. Greetings were exchanged as though they were all well acquainted, Jarod's hand once more resting on the woman's back as he tipped his head, laughing at something another guy said.

My focus dropped to his fingers against the blue satin of

the woman's dress, remembering too well how he'd brought me to climax time and again, how he'd sucked my cum from them.

Shivers raced over my skin even as claws wanted to sink from my knuckles like Wolverine's blade so I could go slice a bitch. Jealousy swirled like a noxious brew in my gut. Something I had no right to feel but couldn't stop from churning my insides.

"Want another beer?"

Tearing my focus off Jarod and his...*friend*, I flashed a smile at Jackson. His teeth gleamed pearly white from a gorgeous shade of ebony skin. Add in the golden hue to his eyes, the black, curly lashes framing them, and the man would have easily been on my radar to gift me a dose of dick —if my brain hadn't been so damn set on the nurse/escort on the other side of the room.

"I'm good, but thanks." I touched his forearm lightly, allowing myself a bit of flirting since it earned me an appreciate third or fourth over by the man, and I needed a serious ego booster. "If you'll excuse me?"

I went to turn away to go take a moment to breathe in the bathroom, but my focus landed on the door once more.

Auntie Sophie had finally arrived—with Rosie holding her hand.

The little angel wore a sparkly pink wig that fell around her shoulders, perfectly matching the bubblegum shade of her dress—the exact color as mine even though I looked putrid in pink. But when Uncle had told me about how his granddaughter had chosen to wear her favorite dress for the party being held in her honor, I hadn't been able to help myself. I'd even opted for a bow atop my shoulder on the single strap holding my dress up to match the one at Rosie's back.

I'd also spoken with her a few days after starting the plans for the event, asking for her input, and she'd chosen the finger foods the waitstaff served off silver trays.

Eyes wide, Rosie glanced around the room as though entranced by the pretty dresses, twinkling lights, and sparkling jewelry of some of Boston's most well-to-do.

I made my way toward her, and the second she caught sight of me, she squealed, ripping her hand from Auntie Sophie's to clap hers together.

"Chrissy!" She was the only one allowed to call me what my mom had before her death.

Eyes stinging, I caught her up in my arms, hugging her tight. "Hey, Princess Rosie. Welcome to your ball."

Chapter 16

Jarod

I wasn't a fan of crowds, but when Mary Rose had insisted me and Doctor Wendy go to her party on Saturday night, I hadn't been able to say no. Especially once her grandpapa had requested we, along with whoever else wasn't on the clock that night, attend the charity event.

While I'd donated thousands to cancer research over the years, I planned to take part in the silent auction he had set up.

When Wendy and I walked into the hotel's ballroom, I'd been staggered by the number of people—and the status of some of those individuals.

A state representative, one senator, a few well-known faces from TV commercials...the list went on after a single sweep of my gaze over the crowd. Luckily, co-workers stood nearby, and we headed toward them, snagging some champagne from a passing waiter on our way.

Within a few minutes, I'd reached my limit of peopleing for the night but stood in place rather than escaping for some much-needed rest and quiet. I'd worked a twelve-hour shift, and even though we'd gotten good news one of our patients going into remission, I was dead on my feet.

Shit would be different if I managed to actually sleep at all the past two weeks.

A childlike squeal sounded behind me, and I turned, grunting as though a truck slammed into my chest.

Christine, the woman who had refused to leave my thoughts bent to scoop Mary Rose up into her arms.

"Jesus," I hissed, rubbing at my pecs, trying to reach the sudden ache inside me.

"She looks adorable," Wendy said from beside me, but I barely heard her voice over the ringing in my ears.

My gaze swept over Christine's curves wrapped up in something...*way* too pink for her skin tone. Blinking, I realized she wore the same color as my favorite little patient. A bow sat atop Christine's shoulder, a perfect match to the one tied behind Mary Rose's back. Tulle even lined beneath both their hems, sweeping away behind them almost like a... mermaid's tail.

Heart beating heavy in my chest, I gazed at the woman who had hit me twice as hard as the first time I'd set my eyes on her. I could feel the draw to move closer. Breathe her into my lungs, infusing my blood once more with the vitality it had been missing since walking away like she'd told me to do after three rounds of the best sex of my life.

"Earth to Jarod." A finger poked me in the side, and I tore my focus off Christine who'd tipped her forehead against Mary Rose's as they spoke quietly to one another.

Wendy smirked at me.

"Hmm?" I asked, my attention firmly focused on my periphery and the girls in pink.

"Either you just got hit by Cupid's arrow, or that champagne you've been sipping is really moonshine like my great grandfather used to still."

I huffed a forced laugh, brushing off Wendy's comment.

She arched a dark eyebrow. "Really? That's how you're playing this? How do you know the woman—and who is she?"

"Christine Gemberling," a deep voice I recognized answered before I figured out what the fuck to say to my co-worker.

I turned toward Mary Rose's grandpapa. "Bradley," I offered my hand, greeting him with the first name he'd insisted upon.

"Jarod," he stated before welcoming Wendy as well. "Christine is my best friend's daughter. She's the one responsible for making this event happen." Pride laced his voice. "Two weeks—that's all the time I gave her, and she came through regardless of the pressure. She's one hell of a woman. Loyal and loving to a fault."

I turned to find Christine had set the little girl once more on her feet, but their fingers entwined. The siren I'd found to be wild, persistent, and definitely impulsive had a much sweeter side, I realized. One that intrigued the hell out of me even though she'd already sunk her wiles beneath my skin to eat away at my resolve to remain aloof from emotional entanglements.

"How long have you known her?" I heard myself ask, wanting any information I could get since all social media belonging to Christine only portrayed the outgoing side of her, the nightlife she chose to embrace.

Wendy snickered as though well aware of my infatuation, but I ignored her, my focus glued on the lady in pink with her mess of red waves draped over her shoulders and back.

"Since the day she was born," Bradley answered. "I've been best friends with her father since high school."

I longed to beg him to tell me all about her—her family, her passions outside of what she'd shared with me, but I didn't do impulsive in the same way she did. Yes, I desired another night with Christine, fuck knew I wanted a hell of a lot more than that. But not without processing my thoughts and my feelings that pushed to conquer the cool reserve I'd kept in place for my entire adult life.

"She's lovely," I stated the truth of what I thought about the sight of Christine regardless of the horrid dress she wore.

Bradley chuckled and clasped my shoulder. "She's also single and has a weakness for tall, strapping young men such as yourself."

As if her social media hadn't already let me in on that truth.

"That a fact?" I mused quietly, already well aware Bradley didn't lie. Christine had no plans to settle down any more than I did.

And that bit of honest thinking sat strangely heavy on my shoulders.

"Come on," Bradley suggested. "I'll introduce you to her."

I stiffened.

Shit. Fuck. How the hell did I get out of *that?*

Christine led Mary Rose across the ballroom to a group of men I had every intention of eventually making my way toward, men I'd watched on TV the week before when they'd shut down the Buffalo Bills.

"Maybe later," I told Bradley, forcing a smile. "It seems your little angel and her protector will be busy for a while."

The professional athletes knelt down and greeted Mary

Rose, kissing the back of her hand like she was a princess worthy of their worship. Color flushed her usually sallow cheeks, and my eyes stung at their actions. Big, brawny men were brought to their knees by a little girl facing death.

All except for one, anyway—Jackson, the rookie on crutches. His eyes were glued to Christine.

A muscle ticked in my jaw as Christine turned to speak with him, her smile stunning, her hand lightly resting on his arm.

Would he be the one bending her over a piece of furniture later that night? Would he take a slow trip along her body, mapping out the sweet spots that made her moan? Would it be his dick stuffing her full and making her come?

"Goddamnit." I swallowed hard, recognizing and admitting to myself I experienced another first thanks to the flame-haired witch. Jealousy. What an ugly feeling.

Jackson leaned toward her, his hand sliding low on her back, and I bristled. Sure, I'd lightly touched Wendy in the same way when steering her into and across the ballroom, but my intentions were purely platonic in nature, exactly the same she felt toward me.

But that asshole running back?

He wanted Christine. And being who he was, I didn't doubt his ability to get inside her panties.

My body thrummed with tension, and I blocked out the voices around me, the almost too-loud music from the DJ in the opposite corner. Laughter met my ears from my co-workers beside me, but I couldn't tear my focus off Christine and that dick who thought he could put his hands on her...

Christine shivered but not in the same way as when I'd had my hands all up in her space. A slight step to the side rid her of Jackson's touch.

I hadn't been aware Bradley had left my side, but he stepped in, grasping Christine's elbow. She nodded at whatever he said, both of them taking Mary Rose's hands and leading her off to meet someone else.

Thank fucking Christ, because I'd been about ready to lose my shit.

My gaze trailed after Christine, every cell in my body honed in on the woman I'd been dreaming about, and not just while sleeping.

"Is she the one who has your panties all twisted up?"

Blinking, I glanced down at Wendy. "Huh?"

The doc nodded with her chin toward Christine before smirking up at me. "First it's heart eyes, then alpha *get your hands off her or else* energy. And don't tell me I didn't catch the panic on your face when Bradley offered to introduce you. That wasn't insecurity—you don't have an ounce of that in your character. Nope." Wendy popped the P. "That's pure *I already know the woman but can't let that info out* kind of fear. So tell me." Wendy leaned into me, lowering her voice. "How do you know Christine Gemberling?"

As if I'd ever reveal my night job to her.

"Doesn't matter," I tried to brush her off.

Wendy laughed. "I've worked with you for five years, Jarod, so forget trying to hide from me. I'd say that stunning redhead grabbed hold of your balls once, and you're dying for a second go-round."

"I hate you," I muttered.

"I'm not wrong."

"You're *not* wrong," I admitted, my shoulder slumping even further.

Wendy nudged me with her elbow. "Then go get her, tiger." She let out a low growl, almost a reow sound that made me snort with laughter. "Seriously." She pushed at my arm again. "Live a little. After the day we had, you deserve it. Forget all your usual careful plotting and planning before making a decision. Choose to just *be* in this moment and go grab what you want."

Chapter 17

Christine

I didn't turn to watch Jarod and that tiny bitch interact, but I could sense him, caught glimpses of him out of the corners of my eyes as the next half-hour dragged by.

I'd gone from high as a kite to stunned breathlessness. Thrilled to see Rosie appearing so happy and lively, then once more uncomfortable in my own skin thanks to the injured rookie I realized I had zero interest in leading on. His touch on my lower back had shivers of unease through my blood, and I'd never been so thankful for Uncle Bradley in my entire life as he ushered me and his granddaughter away to greet other potential donors.

The three of us separated for a short time, and I tracked Uncle Bradley and Rosie making their way toward the group of people from the children's hospital where Rosie went for treatments. When Rosie caught sight of Jarod, she launched herself at him—and he caught her up into his arms, swinging her around in a circle, tulle fluttering behind her.

I lost my breath as my chest went tight. Ignoring the

guests around me, I stayed focused on his gorgeous smile and how she giggled, holding onto his cheeks as though sharing a special moment.

Turning away would protect my heart, so I tore my focus off the beautiful sight of them together. The ache didn't fade, but I kept a smile on my face, feigning absolute joy when I felt strangely...bereft.

The time drew near for the auction about a half hour later, so I finally excused myself from those around me and approached the DJ, dragging Uncle Bradley along with me. We'd left Rosie with Auntie Sophie and my dad, but I couldn't as easily set aside Jarod's presence from the back of my mind.

I'd been too aware of him since his arrival, and there was no way he'd missed me in the shifting people around us. Unable to meet his gaze or even intentionally look for him, I kept my eyes to myself. Pretended I didn't notice him, let alone yearned for him with a stomach-quaking need that made me feel weak and jittery.

Talking to Jarod, breathing in the citrus spice of his cologne, would only make me crave more of whatever it was that had drawn us so closely together two weeks earlier. Knowing it was best to keep away from him didn't make the choice easy though.

Had we been in a smaller crowd, a quieter setting, I didn't doubt the draw would reel us both in, and make us face shit I felt sure he didn't want to think about either.

Uncle Bradley accepted the mic from the DJ as he turned down the music, and I stood back in the shadows, trying to listen to Rosie's grandpapa use his wiles of persuasion on those he'd invited to help in the cause to kick cancer's ass. He negotiated contracts for a living, and the man could wheel and deal.

The silent auction items had been spread on tables around three of the ballroom's four walls, all donated by local businesses in the greater Boston area. It had taken me dozens of phone calls, a couple of hundred miles tacked onto my car's odometer, and even three full days of missing my day job to make the event happen.

But I had.

And now I can rest.

Releasing a slow, steady breath, I sank deeper into the shadows of the heavy drapes covering ceiling-to-floor windows that overlooked Boston's skyline. Hidden in darkness, I finally allowed my eyes free rein and scanned the dense crowd. Over six feet, Jarod should have been easy to spot, but I couldn't find him or the small woman he'd arrived with.

My heart sank even as I told myself it would be best if he'd left. I had no business falling for an escort of all men. He fucked for a living. Hell, he'd probably been balls deep in a half-dozen clients since making my body sing. I wondered how many times he'd gotten that dark-haired woman off.

A low growl slid up my throat as those claws once more wanted to sprout from my hands.

"Hey," a low murmur reached my ears at the same moment a warm touch caused electrical charges to race up my arm.

Without turning, I knew who had snuck up on me.

Adrenaline shot through my system, sending my heartbeat straight to my throat. I swallowed hard and angled to face Jarod. "Hey."

"You aren't surprised to see me." He searched my face as though once more attempting to read my every thought.

"I caught sight of you earlier," I admitted, my insides quaking.

"Why didn't you make your way over to our group and greet us like you've done with everyone else?"

I glanced beyond Jarod, looking for his date, dismissing the fact he sounded jealous as hell. "You seemed quite content with your little brunette. Figured I wouldn't interrupt what might be a good thing."

"You're the only *good thing* I've had in two weeks."

My eyebrows shot up, his serious tone more convincing than his words. Did he mean he hadn't enjoyed his night job since being with me? Or that he hadn't been contracted with any clients since? "So you're what...just eye candy for the night?" I couldn't help but dig a little.

"Wendy is my co-worker, and Bradley extended an invite to us."

I bit my tongue to point out that his hands on Wendy didn't look so platonic to me.

A slow smirk curled his lips as though he read my mind. "You're jealous."

"I'm not," I stated, my chin lifting slightly. Better that than call him out in return and prove he spoke the truth.

Jarod leaned close, his exhale ghosting over my ear. "Liar. I see the same emotions on your face that I experienced when Jackson got all up in your personal space."

My eyelids fluttered shut as a shiver rippled over me. Goose bumps rose along my arms and legs in its wake. "I don't want him," I murmured, not sure why I attempted to soothe Jarod when nothing but sex would ever be the only option between us.

"I could tell, but that's not helping my issue."

I pulled back to meet his dark, probing eyes. Like a bubble settled around us, outside noise faded. I could hear my heartbeat thrumming in my ears, could taste the sweetness on his exhales, could literally feel the electrical charges zapping in the inches separating our bodies.

Jarod's gaze dropped to my mouth, and he stroked his thumb along my jawline. "You've bewitched me, Christine, and I don't know what to do about it."

I huffed a snort, his description identical to how I felt about him. "It's called insta-lust. Chemistry," I attempted to brush whatever it was between us off as nothing special.

His focus once more raised to my eyes, sending a rush of warmth between my thighs. "Is that all this is, Christine?"

I couldn't answer.

"Keeping cool, being in control while making decisions, is something I pride myself in," Jarod stated quietly, grasping the side of my neck with his warm palm and tempting me to melt into his touch. "But something about you calls to the wildness inside me. Nothing has drugged me in such a way, not even living the life of an escort where I allow that part of myself its freedom. I do my research before making a plan or decision about people—for very good reason."

"Your parents," I offered what I expected lay behind his careful nature.

Jarod nodded, his thumb stroking beneath my ear sending another shiver down my spine.

"My dad is that way because of my mom," I stated quietly.

Silence settled between us for a few seconds as I ignored his soft touch and worked out the difference between Jarod and I. He chose heedful consideration in life while I'd gone the opposite due to my childhood trauma. I wanted to ask him what he thought about the undeniable connection between us. I wondered how he felt about the draw to set aside his fears and his stance to only live in the moment beneath a contract that would protect his emotions.

The struggle lay in his eyes, one I felt all too strongly—but the memories of Dad's sobs, the utter devastation the loss of his lover had inflicted on his heart lay like a boulder in my mind.

Swallowing against thickness wanting to close off my throat, I tipped my chin up, grasping for the cold inner bitch I desperately needed at that moment. "I feel the sparks between us, Jarod, and I've ignited beneath the flames of your passion, but all fires burn out."

Leaving nothing but ruination and death behind.

Jarod dropped his hold from my neck and stepped back. Reading him came easily since I experienced the same disappointment, the same yearning to prove that the truth I spoke wasn't reality. He might not have witnessed the sorrow I had, my reasons for being so set against allowing love to control my heart, but he'd seen enough as a child.

Some wounds just couldn't be overcome.

Chapter 18

Jarod

My phone rang at ten in the morning after I'd worked an overnight shift at the hospital. Cursing myself for not turning on the do not disturb feature on my cell, I rolled to grab the damn thing off my bed stand.

I didn't recognize the number but was annoyed enough to answer anyway. "This better be fucking good," I growled and lay back again, too bleary-eyed to keep my eyes open.

"Is this Jarod?"

Her sweet voice didn't fool me any. The last fucking thing I needed was a spammer, and I was just pissy enough to mess with the bitch. "Unless you're selling nipple clamps and vibrators, you can fu—"

"This isn't a sales call." The voice snickered. "This is Jessica Lindy. Reid's girlfriend."

"Oh, shit." I attempted to blink myself awake. "Sorry."

She laughed again.

"Everything okay?" I asked, wondering why the fuck Reid's girl would be calling me when she didn't know me from Adam.

"Yes. I just wanted to chat for a few minutes if you have time?"

"Sure." I swung my legs over the side of the bed and leaned forward, trying like hell to wake up enough that I wouldn't just hear but understand whatever she'd called about. "What's up?"

"Christine."

My insides twisted tight. It had been three weeks since the night she'd shut me down when I'd been ready to take a chance. I'd never experienced such pain in my chest—not even when she'd coldly suggested I leave her apartment. While she hadn't been as frosty the night at the fundraiser, I recognized the icy interior beneath her freckled skin I still longed to touch. Taste.

"What about her?" I asked, my tone rough from the lack of sleep.

"Her birthday is Wednesday, and I was wondering if you'd be interested in a second go-round with her."

Christine and I already had more than two helpings of each other, but I knew what Jessica meant. I huffed a sarcastic laugh, although my cock liked the idea of burying inside Christine's lush body again. "She kicked me out after our first night together."

"She also explained how she shut you down at Mary Rose's ball."

My chest tightened as memories flooded my head. The matching pink dresses. The love and affection Christine had shown the little girl. The freeze-out that had burned me more than flames ever could.

"Look," Jessie stated with a sigh when I didn't respond, "the woman likes her freedom and enjoys the single life, but something about you threatened that—in a good way."

"I don't do relationships," I muttered what I'd been

reminding myself every time Christine and the desire for *more* crossed my mind. Nothing lasted—she hadn't lied with that fire analogy she'd dismissed me with. She'd experienced firsthand knowledge of both ends of that tragic event. Loss and heartache.

"Neither does she—or so she says," Jessie replied. "Personally, I think you're both full of shit and are perfect for each other."

Did Jessie not know about how Christine's mom died and how it had traumatized her? How was it possible Christine had told me and not one of her best friends?

"No offense, but you don't even know me," I stated rather than asking and possibly being pushed to share a story that wasn't mine to tell.

"No, but Reid does."

I scratched the stubble along my jaw. "So that's why my ears have been ringing a lot lately," I muttered.

Jessica laughed again. "They should have been. Look"— her voice turned serious—"Christine is a great catch. She just hasn't found the right guy yet."

"And you think I'm that man?"

"Let's just say that I know Christine, and if she says you're scary as hell, dangerous with a capital D, then she's thoroughly intrigued."

"Could just be that our night was something out of her norm," I offered. "I'm the unattainable paid escort. That would intrigue half of the female population."

"Reid was also 'unattainable' at one time."

Jessie had me there.

"If you need more proof," she continued, "Christine hasn't gone out with anyone else since meeting you, and she's not the type to sit at home on weekends let alone five in a row."

Fuck. Me.

I scrubbed a hand over my face, refusing to acknowledge the hope that swelled inside my chest. "Goddamnit," I muttered to myself.

"So, are you as interested as she told me your eyes claimed after that slow, torturous fuck in her bed, or was that just part of the job of satisfying a client?"

"Women talk too much," I grumbled, slumping an elbow onto my knee. Just the memory of the connection between us in that moment made every muscle in my body weak as fuck. Desperate as hell.

"We absolutely do. So, are you?"

"What else did Christine say?" I asked rather than answering Jessie, staring at my closed blinds and the line of sunlight peeking through either side.

"She said you gave her *that* look, one that made her heart stop and then flood with a feeling she's never experienced before."

"Those were her exact words?" I asked, my damn smile stretching even though I didn't want it to.

"Close enough."

"Shit." The woman was simply scared shitless—same as me. I could work with that.

"So will you do it?" Jessie asked.

"Elite will have to charge you," I stated since simply showing up at Christine's wouldn't help sway her my way. If I'd been *hired*, however...she was too damn loyal to waste her friend's money.

Jessie sighed as though she'd been hoping I'd offer to do her friend for free. "Fine, but on the day you move in together, I want a refund."

I chuckled, hoping to get to that point but highly

doubting it considering Christine's stubbornness. "Deal," I agreed. "What did you have in mind?"

"She told me that she confessed her number one fantasy to you."

A grin curled my lip upward. "She's got an exhibitionist streak."

"If I was a nicer friend, I'd offer Reid's eyes for the evening, but that man is mine."

I chuckled. "He wouldn't agree to it anyway. He *is* all yours."

"Think you can find a willing participant to sit in a dark corner and watch the two of you?"

Just the idea of how turned on Christine would be turned on by a peeping Tom got my blood heading southward. "On a Wednesday night? Absolutely."

"Perfect. So, who do I need to contact to set this in motion?"

I pushed up off the bed and headed for the kitchen and a bottle of water, rattling off Dina's direct phone number. "One last add-on to our little agreement—if all I get out of this is a broken heart, you pay me double."

"You got it," Jessie answered without hesitation.

I huffed an incredulous chuckle. "You're convinced she won't kick me out of heaven, aren't you?"

"She swallowed the hook along with whatever you baited her with. All you need to do is reel her in."

I grabbed a cold bottle of water from my fridge. "Enjoy fishing, do you?"

"No, but the lure fits."

I outright laughed.

A few seconds later, I crawled back into bed, hopeful and wary all at once. I hadn't agreed to fuck any clients for Elite in the weeks since I'd met Christine. Three times I'd acted as eye candy, but Micah had started to give me shit about needing to hire a replacement for my dick.

Closing my eyes, I told myself that if Christine wouldn't bend her stance on taking a chance with me, I would walk away for good. But I would have one last taste, a final memory to remember her by...it would have to be enough.

Then afterward?

I would find a way to get back to the closed-off life I'd lived before she entered my life like a wrecking ball, making me wish for things I never thought I would want.

Chapter 19

Christine

Birthdays sucked ass.

The big 3-0 had struck, and I refused to celebrate aging, even threatened Dad against holding any type of surprise party. I'd already plucked two gray hairs from above my left ear, and when I frowned, a line indented the once smooth skin between my eyebrows. I even had a fucking age spot on my left temple.

At thirty!

"Fucking hell," I whined to myself while peering into the fogged mirror above my bathroom sink. Using my fingertips, I pulled back and tightened the skin of my cheeks. Auntie Sophie had a facelift a few years earlier—it'd done wonders in removing a few years' worth of sag and wrinkles. I turned my head side to side. Doing the same would probably change the appearance of my eyes though. They would end up all squinty, and with my luck, everyone and their mother would know I'd had work done.

Pride came before vanity in my brain.

Expelling a huff of air, I grabbed my empty wineglass off the tub's side where I'd spent the last half hour soaking and sipping some merlot, trying to forget about the work day from hell. It was time for a refill, and I would spend the rest of the evening like a hermit in front of my TV watching some stupid reality show about people finding love.

The towel wrapped around my body and tucked between my breasts sagged as I poured another drink, my gaze flitting to the island.

"Fucking *hell*," I muttered again, lifting my glass. I hadn't gone out since that night I'd met Jarod. I had zero desire to meet anyone, let alone feel fingertips on my skin that didn't belong to him. I swallowed down two big gulps of the dry wine. Forget fucking anyone else either.

"What the hell is wrong with you?" I asked myself while topping off my wine and emptying the bottle.

My doorbell rang.

Growling over having my pity party interrupted, I strode toward my door and peephole that allowed me to check who visited before I decided if I wanted to actually be home or not since my car sat hidden in my garage. At least the exterior lights illuminated who stood on my front porch.

The limo driver from Elite, his black hair slicked back in a ponytail.

"Holy..." I cleared my throat as a thrill shot through me, but I hesitated from opening the door. Perhaps the dude was a perv and wanted a piece of what Jarod had gotten. Wracking my brain for why else the driver would be there, I came up with the only obvious other reason. Someone had bought me a birthday present.

The chain still attached, I turned the knob and peeked out through the three-inch crack, my towel-wrapped body hidden behind the door. I parted my lips to ask him what he wanted, but he held up a card, smirking as I read the three simple words.

Happy Birthday – Jessie

My gaze jerked back up to his face, and I blinked as I drummed up his name from my slightly buzzed brain. *Ricky —that's it.* "Who do you have the pleasure of driving around this evening, Ricky?"

"Just you, Miss Gemberling, but Jarod will meet you at our destination."

I swallowed against the dryness in my throat. "I don't think that's a good—"

"Jessie suggested I mention a certain fantasy if you declined to accept her gift."

Oh, holy fuck. I wanted to kill my friend. I also wanted to kiss her.

"I'm to drive you to the hotel up the road a bit for a clandestine meeting—if you wish to join them."

Them.

Heat flushed through me from head to toe, and my underarms prickled. So not just Jarod. Someone else hiding in the shadows who was meant to go nameless, exactly like the fantasy I'd spilled to Jessie months earlier.

To accept or not? What a loaded question. While I'd denied myself another taste of Jarod that night at the fundraiser, the situation I faced was transactional. Jarod's time and body had been paid for, and if nothing else, the man *was* a professional.

Hell, he was a lot more than that. And with how he was

cautionary before making decisions, I knew he hadn't agreed to the evening without having thought it through.

Jarod would aim to please—and keep his heart just as guarded as mine.

"I-I'll be down in five," I finally said, my tone breathless with the need ramping up inside me.

Ricky smiled and nodded. "Take your time, Ms. Gemberling. My limo is at your disposal until eight tomorrow morning."

Oh. My. God. I shut the door and guzzled my glass of wine, gaze aimed at but unfocused on the peephole.

A tremor shuddered down through me, and I forced my feet to move. My hands shook while I riffled through the clothes hanging in my closet. Teeth holding onto the inside of my lower lip, I yanked out an off-the-shoulder silk shift in blue and a tight, silver minidress. Elegant or slutty?

I let out a snort of huffed laughter and hung the first outfit back up.

Thank fuck I'd lathered all the lady bits and shaved while relaxing in the tub. I dropped the towel and stepped into the mini, shimmying it up over my hips. The damn thing was snugger than the last time I'd worn it a couple of months earlier. Clingy material never paired well when you carried around fat cells that multiplied like bunnies.

Glowering, I yanked the dress back down. "Blue shift it is."

The silken material fell mid-thigh, and I turned in front of my full-length mirror, loving how the sheath's material actually hid the parts of me I didn't care for.

Panties or no panties?

I nibbled my lower lip while perusing through my bureau's top drawer.

Jarod would probably just rip them from my body. I

hoped he would...and that the stranger in the room with us would enjoy watching Jarod's desperation to get them off me.

Face hot and core priming for action at the thought, I grabbed a black, lacy thong and headed into the bathroom. While a full face painting with smoky eyes would better fit an evening out, I opted for a few licks of mascara, blush, and pale lip gloss, the same as I'd gone for on our first night together.

I unclasped the clip from my hair and shook my head, running my fingers through the thick waves left over from work. Long red tresses curled over my shoulders, and my face appeared virginal with its barely there makeup, but the spark in my eyes betrayed the arousal flooding through me.

The red flag warning of danger in the back of my mind did nothing to make me pause. Having another chance to enjoy Jarod in a safe environment?

Fuck yes, please and thank you, Jessie.

Giddy and pulse trilling, I grabbed a small purse, threw in a few necessities, and typed a quick text to my friend.

Me: **I can't even right now...**

Her reply zipped through before I made it to my front door.

Jessie: **I want all the juicy details.**

Smirking, I sent three thumbs up rather than get into the whole "How the hell can you afford this" conversation.

I pulled open my door, and Ricky did a quick once-over down my body and back up, his gaze not lingering long enough to creep me out. "You look lovely."

Beaming, I accepted his outstretched arm. "Why, thank you, Ricky."

My knees knocked, and my pulse raced. I couldn't stop grinning either.

"Nervous?" Ricky asked while leading me down my stoop's stairs.

"Yes."

He chuckled and patted my hand clutching at his elbow. "Mr. Zimmerman and Mr. Fox will take good care of you."

Mr. Fox...Jarod's best friend and Elite's owner if I remembered correctly.

Oh, good God. The thought of a serious professional watching me brought back to life all my aging and weight insecurities. "Mr. Fox as in Elite's owner?" I managed to whisper.

"Yes."

"I-I don't know..."

Ricky opened the limo's back door for me. "Ms. Gemberling." He smiled again but didn't insist I climb in. "Mr. Fox is just another guy—"

I snorted.

"—who enjoys satisfying his customers like any of his other escorts."

Huffing a sigh, I glanced down over my dress and heels choice.

"As I said before, you look lovely."

I lifted my head and met Ricky's kind, smiling eyes.

"Any man would be honored to act as your escort—or watch you this evening."

Flutters took over my stomach again as I inhaled as much oxygen as I could.

"Okay." I strode forward and climbed into the limo, my insides jumping. "Sneak me away to my secret rendezvous."

Chapter 20

Jarod

Of course, Micah would be the only guy available to act as a voyeur for the night. I'd requested Cooney, but he'd been asked to do a Shibari demonstration over at that BDSM club where he finally admitted to being a patron.

"They're en route."

I stopped my pacing to turn toward Micah, rubbing my hands down over my gym shorts.

His cool gaze studied me from the corner of the seating area where he lounged in a plush chair, cell in hand. "Are you sure about this, Zimmerman?"

I'd admitted after our getting together for that Pats/Steelers game weeks earlier that I was good and truly fucked over Christine just like Cooney and Sean had suggested.

Micah had known me long enough that he understood my thought processes. I didn't make decisions without giving them thorough consideration. So why was he questioning my agreeing to another round with a woman who claimed to not want me?

"I have to make sure that connection I felt with her is real," I explained. "I want to look into her eyes when she allows me to sink into her body. I *need* the verification that there is something potent between us—one way or another."

She'd admitted freely to feeling those same sparks I did, to igniting from my touch, but it had been so much more than a raging fire between us. There was a steady draw, a yearning so goddamn deep it made my chest ache.

"And if she denies you once this fantasy of hers plays out?" Micah asked.

"Then you'll get your tall, dark, and handsome back on Elite's menu," I stated quietly even though the idea of pleasuring another woman, even laying hands on one, threatened my esophagus with the need to hurl.

Lips pursed, Micah eyed me, eventually nodding. "I hope she's your soulmate."

I blinked. "Huh?"

"I said I hope Christine is your person, Jarod."

My throat went tight. "Seriously?" I asked, my tone ragged.

"You've been miserable every time we've gotten together over the past couple of weeks, but when you talk about her, your face lights up with some sort of inner glow. It's creepy as shit, but I'll admit it's a good look on you."

My insides actually melting a bit, I shot him a grin. "She's fucking amazing. Gorgeous. Fiery. So damn driven and stubborn." I chuckled, the memory of her tilted chin and flashing eyes making my dick twitch in my shorts.

"Yeah, yeah, yeah." Micah waved a hand while rolling his eyes. "I get it."

He didn't really—but maybe one day he would. "Someday, Micah..."

"Nope. No fucking way."

"That's what I always used to say, but something about this girl just captured my focus."

"She's got you by the balls, you mean," he scoffed.

"That too, and I'm okay with it."

"You will be until she kicks your ass out again," Micah argued.

"Fuck." I scowled at my friend, crossing my arms. "Why are you such a Donnie Downer?"

"Because I know better than to allow my head to float in the clouds. Now—" he kicked back and crossed his ankles "—your client will be here shortly. You'd best set the mood and ready yourself to earn your pay."

Barefoot and dressed only in shorts, I planned to play the part of horny boyfriend waiting to surprise his woman when she got home from work. I wasn't supposed to be aware of the guy lurking in the shadows—the seating area of the suite we'd rented for the night promised Micah his own secretive little corner.

Christine and I both would easily see him if we looked in his direction, but I planned to keep her occupied. And if she truly wished to play out the fantasy, I expected she would pretend he didn't exist even while the truth he did burned her up inside.

Without a doubt, she would be hot for a thorough fucking before she even walked through the door. I could imagine the slickness between her thighs, how ready she would be to climax at the slightest touch.

I shut down the overheads near Micah, leaving the dimmers above the bed on low. Enough light shone to ensure Christine wouldn't lose her way.

Ricky would give her a key card to enter. She would have to make the choice to unlock the door and willingly cross the threshold. While Christine claimed to love dick, she wouldn't have agreed to meet with me unless she wanted mine again. Either she thought herself emotionally strong in the midst of the glowing embers I planned to rain down on her, or she craved me as much as I did her.

Hope had fused through me at Ricky's text telling Micah she'd accepted Jessie's gift and sat in the back of the limo. We'd been under the agreement that he would name the Elite Christine was meeting even if she didn't ask which man would be at her beck and call for the evening.

I wanted her to know who waited for her since Jessie had told me in advance she'd planned to keep the gift a secret until Ricky showed up at her door. Jessie had promised having to make a rash decision would land Christine in my arms.

And so far, it seemed as though she'd been right.

Once I had a playlist pulled up on my cell, I linked it to the speaker I'd brought along. I checked again on the black bag alongside the bed and the supplies I'd already laid out on the bed stand.

Other than stripping out of the shorts I wore, I was prepared for Christine's arrival. Emotionally, I wasn't sure I was quite ready for what the night would bring, but I'd never been one to shirk away from a challenge.

Blowing out a slow, steady exhale, I went into the bathroom, lights out, and the door slightly cracked open. While I had no wish to jump out and scare Christine, I had every intention of prohibiting her from turning tail and leaving. Yes, if she said stop, I wouldn't hesitate to do so—but I remembered how she'd been tempted to melt at my touch at Mary Rose's ball, how she'd sagged against my chest from pressing against her body on the dance floor all those weeks ago.

A shudder ripped through me, and my half-hard cock

I'd been dealing with all day at work thickened fully at the memory of her curves plastered to mine. Even with clothing separating us, Christine had felt divine.

"She's on her way up." Micah let me know he'd gotten another text from Ricky, and I shook out my hands at my sides as adrenaline coursed through my blood.

I was nervous as hell, and my dick refused to be held back in its desire to return home inside her warmth.

Breathing deeply, I shoved off my shorts. How the hell things had felt so right after only spending a few hours with Christine, I had no clue. But I'd stopped questioning the emotions that night when Wendy had encouraged me to give Christine another shot.

This is the last one, I told myself, but the sound of a muffled beep—the room's door unlocking—stole my thoughts.

Hesitant steps brought Christine into view through the propped-open bathroom door. She didn't glance my way, her focus on the king-sized bed straight ahead.

Even in darkened profile, the appearance of her hit me with that slam to the chest, and I bit back a groan.

What was it about her that made me fucking crazy with want beyond mere lust?

Squeezing the base of my hard dick, I imagined how the night would transpire as if willing the universe and any greater beings in existence to make things happen according to my desires.

Here we go...

Chapter 21

Christine

A quick scan of the bedroom revealed it sat empty, and I couldn't hear anyone else breathing over the quiet music drifting from the area straight ahead. Light shone down dimly from above the bed like a beacon in the darkness, drawing me forward.

Moth to a flame.

I'd mentally prepared my buzzed brain for the scorching fire that would without doubt erupt inside the hotel room, but my need for dick and the promise of a man who knew how to use his ended up trumping all other thoughts.

I wanted Jarod—at least, I admitted to my body's desire.

My heart was another matter altogether. Pushing against that strange attachment, that deep-seated yearning for promises of forever, roses, and sharing pillow talk, I stepped quietly into the room, allowing the door to click shut behind me.

Wishing to stay in the moment and enjoy my fantasy come to life to the fullest, I slipped off my heels and quietly placed my small purse on the countertop outside the bathroom. My focus still on the large bed and its pale coverlet and plump pillows, I moved deeper into the darkness.

Awareness skittered over my skin. In my periphery, I could see a man sitting in the far, shadowed corner facing me. Making a note of blond hair, I took a couple more steps, thinking Jarod waited for me somewhere inside the bedroom area I couldn't see from my vantage point.

Warmth caressed my backside for a split second before a recognizable citrus cologne flooded my senses.

"Happy birthday, sweet girl," Jarod murmured against the skin beneath my ear as his body pressed along my back. His hot breath made the hairs on my nape rise, and I fought to stay upright as a small moan passed my lips.

"Thank you," I managed as my heart raced in anticipation and fear alike.

I'd forgotten how potent his presence was, how his warmth, his touch, enticed me to submit to his every whim. I tensed to run as the fight or flight instinct kicked in, but Jarod slid the sheath's strap off my shoulder, sending my dress floating down to pool around my ankles, leaving me in nothing but my thong.

The man on the chair shifted.

"Christine..." Jarod groaned my name while running his large hands down my arms, back over the curve of my ass, and around to my rib cage. Filling them with the heaviness of my breasts, he lifted them as though in offering to our shadowed observer.

Electrical current swept through to my clit as Jarod pinched my pebbled nipples and pressed his very naked body against my backside. I fought the need to arch as the hard ridge of his cock fit against the crack of my ass cheeks.

"So damn beautiful," he whispered, his lips nipping at

my lobe as he thumbed over my suddenly aching nipples. Shockwaves rippled down between my thighs.

I gasped, twitching in his hold and yet sagging at the same time.

"So responsive," he murmured, sending a complete body shiver through my system.

His hands followed the path still tingling from chest to thighs where he cupped my core in his firm grip. He had to feel how wet I already was through the thin material separating our skin "I need to taste this heavenly bit of flesh," he whispered in my ear, my eyelids fluttering shut. "Do you want it slow and torturous or hard and fast?"

Jarod's murmured words along my neck slammed memories of our last time together through my brain, weakening my knees. "I-I don't care. I just need to come." I sounded like a breathless porn whore desperate for the hard cock grinding against my ass.

Rather than pressing his fingers into me and bringing me to climax right there on the spot, Jarod stepped back, leaving me cold.

I turned my head, needing to see his face.

Undeniable need poured from his dark eyes, and fuck my heart for wanting to lay itself on a platter for him to devour. He palmed my cheek, that damn soft pad of his thumb reeling my mind as it smoothed back and forth over my cheekbone.

"Christine..."

I pressed a hand against his bare chest until he blinked the desire to make love to my mouth from his stare.

"No kissing," I whispered.

He shut down, all trace of emotion dissolved from his face. I recognized the impersonal gaze he'd given me before fucking my ass while I'd bent over my kitchen island. "If that's your wish."

"It is."

"Do I have permission to kiss you elsewhere?" he asked, hand sliding around my hip, fingers dipping inside my panties to slide through my wetness.

I swallowed against the dryness claiming my mouth and widened my legs slightly, hoping he would put his fingers inside me. "Yes."

He dropped to his knees without hesitation, hooked his fingers on the sides of my thong, and slowly dragged the lace downward. "I can smell your want, Christine."

Oh, God.

I gulped while stepping out of my panties.

Jarod nosed over my aching clit, groaning a curse. One feathered kiss atop where I needed him to suck and flick his tongue, and he stood, leaving me panting, desperate for more.

A harsh crack sounded half a heartbeat before I registered he'd swatted my ass.

"Crawl to the middle of the bed on your hands and knees," Jarod commanded, his tone cool—and alpha-hot as fuck.

I should have bristled, should have been pissed, but his purpose was to bring a fantasy to life. Put on a show. Please a client whose interests he'd asked about the first time he'd fulfilled his obligations.

Swallowing hard at the reminder of what I'd entered into, what I'd *told* myself I only had space in my life for, I obeyed.

The man in the corner shifted as I dropped to my knees, heavy breasts swaying. His hand pressed down on his crotch.

Jesus...

Eyes clenching shut, I attempted to calm my racing heart and heightened breaths. Unsure of myself for the first time in forever, I glanced back at Jarod.

"If it's too much, tell me to stop, and I will," he said, concern flitting through his gaze over my hesitation.

He had said almost those exact words to me once before, but any thoughts of saying no to whatever he wanted to do to me was extinguished by the need swelling inside me. I wanted him. Badly, if the moisture smearing between my thighs was any indication.

"Go on." Jarod feathered his fingertips against my backside, prodding me to move forward. "Get up there on that bed and lift your lush ass to me in offering. I'm going to eat you out until you come all over my tongue, then I'll fuck you into that mattress until you're begging me to let you come again."

Holy fuck, fuck, fuck.

Heat flashed through me at Jarod's words and the fact a man sat in the shadows listening. Watching.

I moved forward, the feeling of both men's stares searing and pebbling my skin. On hands and knees, I did as Jarod had ordered, all sense of self-consciousness blowing right out the door as I fully submitted myself to their perusal—chest down, ass up, and thighs spread.

The bed dipped behind me, and my eyelids fell shut as Jarod buried his face in my sopping pussy. Same as the first time he'd gone down on me, he dove in like a starved man, lapping, nosing, and teeth grazing as though desperate for my taste on his tongue.

"Oh, fuck," I whimpered, giving in to the need to lift my ass higher by arching my back into a deep bend.

Jarod grasped my cheeks and spread me wider, his

thumbs digging into my flesh. "So fucking delicious." He dove back in with a groan, licking me from clit to asshole where he lingered, rimming me in slow torturous circles and gentle probes.

Curses spilled from my lips, and I couldn't decide which of my two holes I needed him to wreck. Lewd wet sounds rose as Jarod feasted, and my moans and whimpers fought him for dominance.

A hiss sounded, a noise that hadn't come from either of us.

My eyelids lifted.

Micah, Elite Escort's owner, sat in my direct line of sight. He had pulled his cock free of his pants and slid a hand down to the base, blue eyes locked on the live porn action in front of him.

The man had one gorgeous, thick cock...he was fucking huge.

Jarod slid two fingers deep inside of my pussy as his tongue pressed into my ass, rolling my eyes back into my head.

"Shit," I whispered, shifting my hips to fuck myself against his touch. Same as the first time, Jarod worked my body without a road map, fingers twisting to rub along the front of my vaginal wall and finding my happy button like it had been waiting for him.

My climax ripped through me unexpectedly, and I cried out, my pussy clenching at his fingers, the ring of muscle in my ass around his probing tongue.

Groans from both men reached my ears as I panted through the waves rippling through my body. "Fuck... Oh, fuck, Jarod." The words poured from my parted lips as I ground my pussy against his face, my need far from sated.

He continued to stroke me, and a second climax burned through my pussy, clenching at his hand.

"Jesus!" I gasped, shuddering hard enough I slid forward onto the bed.

Jarod lapped at my cum, a deep growl rumbling from his chest. "Sweet as honeysuckle," he said against my throbbing lower lips.

My toes and fingertips tingled, and the muscles in my body slackened beyond what any hot bath could do. I needed more, and this time wasn't above begging.

"Give me your dick, Jarod. Please."

Chapter 22

Jarod

I glanced over at Micah as I lifted my head from the sweetest-tasting pussy I'd ever buried my face in. He stroked his huge cock, gaze glued to Christine spread out before me.

Unease tingled down my spine. I didn't like him looking at her...enjoying the sight of her lush curves.

She's not yours. She doesn't desire you like that.

Her eyes while stopping me from kissing her had said it all. The cold reminder did little to lessen my jealousy or the painful throbbing in my cock. She lusted for me to bury balls deep inside of her while another man watched, which I wasn't too keen on, but, fuck, did I want her. To make love to her mouth, to her body, to keep her all to myself. Hide her away in my bedroom, tied to my bed so that no other man could touch or look at her.

The desires in my head scared the shit out of me, even more so since I knew Christine's didn't align with mine.

Fucking screwed, Cooney had said. He was so damn right.

I told myself to pretend Micah wasn't here, to satisfy the customer as I'd been paid to do.

A muscle in my jaw ticking, I grabbed the items I'd thrown on the bed beside us. A quick condom rolled on, and I yanked Christine up by her hair so she rested against my chest, her tits jutting out.

"You're going to use that heavenly pussy of yours to make me come," I whispered against her ear and bit on her lobe.

She gasped and nodded but didn't reach for where I held tight to her hair.

"Get on my dick, sweet girl."

She arched her back in offering. Groaning, I pulled her down by her hair and slammed up with my hips to bury myself deep, denying myself the opportunity to watch her expression as I sank into her.

A low groan ripped from my throat as the heat of her core bled through the condom. "You're so fucking tight. So damn perfect."

I spread my legs, pulling hers wide along with mine, putting her on full display for the chair in the corner—just like she'd fantasized about.

Christine whimpered and gyrated her hips, grinding on my cock. I sat still, making her work for it, my hand still tangled in her long auburn waves. She moved like she danced, all sensual fluidity, a sweet siren intent on tangling me in her web.

Didn't she know I'd already been caught? That I'd sucked down her witch's brew she had offered like a poisoned apple?

But did a happily ever after lay at the end of our story?

I hoped for it. Lusted after it. Fucking needed it like my next breath regardless of how she shielded herself from me.

Heart racing, I slid my lips along her collarbone, angling her head back so I could see her face. Lips parted and eyes hooded, she continued to writhe as though every gyration of her hips, every squeeze of her inner walls around my hard length, would tie my soul tighter to hers.

"You love riding my dick," I murmured and slid my other hand to her soft belly, pinkie teasing over her mound.

"God, yes!" Christine blinked, her gaze flitting to the chair in the corner.

"What's he doing?" I asked, hating that I wanted to know.

She gasped as I feathered a fingertip over her erect clit. "J-jerking himself."

My dick bucked inside her, and I made a deep noise of appreciation I hadn't felt until that moment. Christine was on me. Mine for the night. That initial sense of jealousy faded, my insides settling. "Do you like that he's getting off while watching you fuck yourself on my cock?"

Christine licked her lip and nodded, a shiver shifting her in my hold.

"Do you want him to come over here and touch you?" I whispered against her ear, hating that I needed to know if her fantasy included me sharing her with another man.

Her lower lip disappeared between her teeth, and my heart seized at the thought she deliberated. She shook her head though, and my breath left in a rush.

Thank fuck.

I thrust up to meet her, and her eyes shut, a whimper once more parting her lips. "You're so fucking gorgeous, and this pussy..." I groaned, burying deep inside her. "So wet." I thrust again. "Hot."

Christine moaned, and I slid my touch lower to cup where I impaled her, slickness smearing over my fingers.

I hissed at how intensely my balls throbbed for release. Needing a breather, I stilled and lifted my hand. "Taste how much your body craves me, how good we are together."

She hesitated, her eyelids popping open, but she stared at my fingers—not Micah.

I tightened my grip on her hair. "Do it."

The tip of her tongue darted out and licked the top of my middle finger.

"More," I said, stabbing up as hard as I could, jolting her body on my cock.

She closed her mouth over the two fingers I offered her and hollowed her cheeks, sucking them clean, her tongue hot on my flesh.

"Christ, Christine," I growled, releasing my hold on her hair to band my arm around her chest. My hips moved without thought, fucking deep inside her heat, my other hand sliding between her splayed thighs. Her clit protruded above swelled labia, her arousal slick and dripping from my balls to the sheet beneath us.

Whimpers leaked from her parted lips, and she arched against my chest.

I thrust deep against her womb, and she gasped, fingernails digging into my forearm as I rimmed where we joined with teasing fingertips.

"Oh, God," she groaned the words as I blatantly ignored her clit. "Fuck me—*touch* me. Please, Jarod."

The way she begged, her wrecked tone...fuck, Christine called out to me on so many levels. A soft whine built in her throat, *please* in repeat whispering past her lips.

Cursing and losing myself to our shared need, I pushed forward, trapping her body beneath me on the bed. My hips jacked, my dick rutting into her in desperation to find completion with her.

"Need you to come for me," I growled into her ear, my arms trapped beneath her curves, fingers seeking to send her flying. "Take me with you."

She gasped and whimpered beneath me, strands of her hair plastered to her sweating cheek and forehead. Her lips parted, and the telltale whine built in her chest.

"Yes," I hissed. "Just like that." I bit at her neck, wanting to be deeper. Lost inside her. "Please."

I pinched her clit hard between my fingers, and she shrieked, her body convulsing beneath me, pussy like a vise around my cock.

Micah grunted from the corner of the room, but I was too far gone to give a shit he got to see how beautifully she released for me.

"Oh, God! Fuck!" She shrieked again as I pinched harder.

My balls seized up, and I gave over to my instincts, sitting up to my knees and yanking her hips off the mattress. I slammed into her tight heat, grunting and groaning with every thrust, wild and out of control on a mission to finish while she pulsed around my cock.

"Fuck!" My taint convulsed, and cum erupted up my shaft, causing stars to burst behind my eyelids. "Goddamn, Christine!"

I clenched my jaw, release pumping through me in throbbing spurts. "Fucking hell," I gasped once finished, a full body shudder unclenching my muscles. Heaving for breath, I opened my eyes, attempting to focus through the haze of euphoria and the woman who'd taken me there.

Christine lay like a corpse beneath me except for the air panting from her mouth, fluttering the strands of hair over her face. Pink fused her cheeks, highlighting the spattering of freckles over her nose. Plump lips, stubborn chin…

A soft smile curved my lips as I slid my palms down her back, hands once more flaring around her wide hips. I'd left bruises on her skin...marked her like a fucking savage. I felt no shame. No remorse.

Swallowing my growl of satisfaction, I loosened my hold and shifted away until my semi slid from her.

A sense of detachment swept over me, and I swallowed hard.

"Okay?" I murmured, staring at her swollen lower lips, wishing like fuck my cum leaked from her well-used pussy so I could shove it back inside where it belonged.

"Mmm hmm." A shiver pebbled her skin as though she too felt the same loss I did.

"I'll get a towel to clean you up," I whispered, backing off the bed. Without glancing at Micah, I stumbled to the bathroom on weak legs.

I'd never lost myself inside a woman like that before. Never ended up feeling...empty after pulling free from the clasp of a warm, wet core.

Fucking screwed didn't even begin to describe what I was.

Lips in a thin line, I took care of the condom and got a warm, wet towel for Christine.

Micah stood outside the bathroom when I turned to exit. I'd been so damn lost in my thoughts I hadn't heard him sneak up on me. Neither of us spoke for a few seconds, his blue eyes searching my face. I didn't bother shielding, just let my friend see how lost I was, how vulnerable my heart sat atop a platter, waiting for Christine's knife.

"Good luck," Micah finally whispered, clasping my shoulder. "I think you're going to need it."

"Yeah," I murmured, expecting he spoke the truth.

I moved past him and strode across the room, aware Micah ran water in the bathroom.

Christine didn't stir as I knelt on the bed beside her and used the washcloth to wipe her clean. She sighed, but that and the lift of her back with each breath was the only indication life pumped through her arteries.

The room's door opened, the latch clicking quietly a few seconds later, leaving us alone.

"Did I hurt you?" I asked quietly, unable to keep from trailing my fingertips down her spine.

The hint of a smile ghosted at the corner of her lips again. "No," she whispered.

"Do you want me to leave?" I held my breath, my heart pounding between my ears.

Christine heaved a sigh and rolled onto her side, passion-hazed eyes peering up at me. "I should, but I don't."

Without giving her a chance to expand on the words, I laid down behind her and pulled her back against me. My arm rested over the dip of her waist, hand splayed on the soft skin beneath her breasts. I wanted to bury my face in her hair and breathe in her honeysuckle scent but kept my face and affection to myself.

We lay in quietness outside the soft music playing in the background, my heart slowing and thumping in time with the beat beneath my palm. The wondering over what went through her mind drove me nuts. I clenched my eyes shut, telling myself to keep my mouth zipped as well.

"So now what?" I heard myself ask as though she'd pulled the words from my lungs with witchery.

She yawned and twined her fingers through mine atop her heart. "I have you until eight tomorrow morning?"

"Yeah."

"Then I want another dose of your dick just as soon as I can move again."

Unable to help myself, I held her close and buried my nose in her hair like I'd wanted to do. "Sounds like a good plan to me."

She drifted off not long after, but my mind wouldn't shut the hell up.

Shifting away and popping on my elbow, I gently pulled Christine onto her back beside me so I could watch her sleep. Little puffs of air escaped her parted lips. Her slightly crooked nose wrinkled as a frown flitted across her brow.

I wondered what went through her mind, what dreams controlled her facial expressions. A wave of hair still stuck to her cheek, and I brushed it free with my fingertips.

Christine sighed and tilted her head toward my hand, seeking out my touch in her sleep. Warmth rushed through me, and I cupped her cheek, staring at her plump lips. I bit down on my tongue to keep from kissing her, from tasting the sweetness of her mouth. Sharing breath. Losing myself even more.

Minutes ticked by...an hour slipped past as I studied her. The curve of her auburn eyebrows, the high cheekbones with their spattering of star-like freckles. Damned pointy chin I wanted to bite. The bow of her top lip I salivated to lick. Her collarbones called out to my teeth too, but I shifted my attention lower to her full breasts and the soft nipples.

Mouth watering and fingers itching to pinch, I lifted higher onto my elbow to better see the rest of her curves sprawled out on display. Her hand rested above the dip of her belly button, smooth skin below leading to the soft patch of trimmed hair between her thighs. A hint of her clit peeked from between the top of her labia, and I fisted my hand rather than touch her.

She shifted, her thigh pressing against my thickened cock. "Mmm."

I lifted my gaze to find her sleepy green eyes peering at me, pupils swelled. She slid her hand between us and wrapped her hand around my hard length. "I want you," she whispered.

A shot of adrenaline slammed into me—I wondered how much, and if she'd meant more than just my body.

Without a word, I rolled on autopilot, settling between her thighs. Heat and wetness pressed against the back of my dick as she wrapped her legs around me, holding me close.

There were no walls, no steel door hiding her from me. She stared up at me with naked honesty and want.

I swallowed hard, wanting to spill the truth in my heart and beg her to let me love her.

She shifted her hips, and I groaned at the tip of my dick enveloped in slick heat. "Fill me, Jarod."

I slid deep inside her warmth without thought. My eyes slid shut, and I rested my forehead against hers, cursing over how good she felt—*too* good.

"Condom. Shit!" I started to pull out, but she clamped me tight to her with her thighs, her ankles locked around my back.

"You get tested all the time, right?" she asked, still unguarded with her gaze, the desire in her emerald orbs stealing my breath.

"Yeah," I rasped. "Got a clean bill of health two weeks ago." I didn't tell her I hadn't been with anyone since her though.

"Me too, and I'm on the pill." Her gaze dropped to my lips. "I want you this way—if you're okay with it."

I bit down on the lip she stared at and pressed back into her body, offering her everything. Full fucking surrender.

Her lips parted with a gasp, eyes flitting back up to mine.

Setting a slow but steady rhythm, I rocked into her wet heat, the slick glide and feel of her inner muscles pulling on my cock enticing me to go deeper. I angled and shifted, giving all I could, gyrating my hips so my pubic bone rubbed against her clit.

She groaned, tipping her head back and baring her neck.

Swooping down, I open-mouth kissed every inch she allowed, flicking my tongue along her skin to taste her.

I'd fucked plenty of women. Pleasured dozens if not hundreds. But I'd never made love, never allowed feelings to dictate how I moved. Sliding my hand between us, I lifted to see her face. "Look at me, Christine."

Her eyelids fluttered open. Huge pupils dominated the green of her irises.

Not bothering to hide the emotion I felt for her from my own gaze, I peered down at her, gently rubbing my fingertips over her clit.

She gasped as I flicked under the hood covering her hard nub, and that whine—God, that fucking *beautiful* sound—rose from her chest and escaped her lush lips as she stared up at me.

"Come around my cock, sweet girl."

A shudder rippled through her pussy, pulling me even deeper, and she arched her back with a moan, keeping her eyes on mine as she went over.

I fell fully in that moment, whispering her name while filling her with my cum.

Chapter 23

Christine

I cracked an eyelid open.

Eight-fifteen, the clock read. But it wasn't my alarm clock. The satin sheets beneath me weren't mine, and the hairy arm and leg draped over my body didn't belong to me either.

Remnants of Jarod's cologne drifted past my nose, and God help me, I smiled and closed my eyes again to relive the night before.

Fantasy number one fulfilled in a way I couldn't have imagined, leaving me sore and sated, but I was more than ready for a second round—

Wait.

Jarod had woken me from hazy sleepiness. I frowned, recalling every emotion filling his dark eyes. I'd wanted to burrow beneath his skin and become one with him, latch onto his soul, and never let go...

Fuck.

I opened my eyes again to find the clock read eight-seventeen.

Our time was up.

Ignoring the ache in my chest, I shifted in his arms, trying to wake him gently. "Hey," I said, keeping my voice low. "Jarod."

"Hmm?" His voice rumbled against my ear, and he squeezed me close.

"You're off the clock."

He rubbed his face against my hair and pushed the mass of waves from my neck. "This isn't about a job right now," he murmured against my skin.

Danger, my mind screamed, but shivers of fire slid down my body as his lips and tongue traced patterns on my neck. I didn't scoot away as I should have. Nope. I had to go and angle my neck to give him better access.

"Mmm, you taste delightful in the morning."

Goddamnit.

I pulled away and sat, lowering my feet to the floor while scanning the room for my dress. There. By the door. Heart thrumming in my throat, I crossed the room, trying to keep the swaying of my ass to a minimum since I felt the heat of Jarod's stare on my backside. I squatted to pick up my dress rather than bending over and giving him a sight he would enjoy too much. Once in the bathroom with the door closed, I shut my eyes and shivered.

That slow rocking of hips the night before had made a huge spider crack in my wall. The look in Jarod's eyes as he'd made love to me, the emotion pouring out of him... We hadn't kissed, but we'd been completely wrapped up in one another regardless. Hell, I'd been desperate for him to take me again. Raw. Nothing between us.

"Goddamnit!" I whispered the word harshly and strode toward the toilet, my insides churning.

He made me weak—want things that scared the shit out

of me. I needed to get the hell out of there to save us both future pain.

I took care of business, yanked up my dress, and ran my shaking fingers through my hair. Anyone with eyes would see the war in mine, the unguarded, vulnerable mess of my mind. *Keep your distance, Christine. Let him touch you again and you're a goner.*

I pulled open the door, hell-bent on escaping the feelings, the desires he stirred up inside me.

Jarod lay on the bed, mussed hair, sleepy and sexy bedroom eyes aimed my way. His gaze flitted down over my state of dress, and a frown tugged on his brow. "You're leaving?"

Somehow, I forced my head up and down in a stilted nod—like my body didn't wish to agree with my mind.

Silence hovered between us, thick with longing, ripe with unease.

I wanted to crawl back beneath that tented sheet and wrap myself around his warm, hard body. I wanted his mouth fused to mine, his cock filling me, erasing everything in my mind but the feel and presence of him. I wanted—no, needed—space between us. Safety.

"I-I wish you all the best," I somehow managed and spun away, grabbing my shoes and bag.

"You *are* my best." Jarod's whisper followed me out the hotel's door.

JE

Fall's cooler nights did nothing to boost my mood like it usually did after a long, hot summer. Everything felt flat— off—since I'd walked out on Jarod. Two more bomb threats worried the Boston area, one including Chantelle's Too, the nightclub where Jarod and I had met. A reporter stood outside the roped-off entrance, explaining how a bomb had been found in one of the lockers.

I sat at the lunchroom table on Friday morning, eating my dry bunny greens and grilled chicken, focusing on the TV across the tiny room.

Footfalls came from the hallway, and Dad appeared in the doorway a few seconds later.

"They found the bomb," I said, my attention flitting back to the reporter as I speared my fork into my salad.

"Thank goodness it didn't go off last night."

I hummed my agreement around my mouthful of boring lunch. Calorie counting sucked ass, but everything had since that night. Shoving aside thoughts of Jarod, his bare cock throbbing, releasing inside me, and the desire to burrow inside his heart, I focused on the present.

"That place has been packed every time I've been there," I said as Dad settled into the chair beside me with his cold pastrami sandwich.

"Hopefully, they'll find something to lead them to whoever is causing this mess."

The reporter went on to state how the threats didn't seem to be making much impact on Boston's nightlife. Businesses stayed open, and customers continued to spend their money, looking for an escape from the day jobs and responsibilities of life.

"I think it would be best if you stayed away from the bars and dance clubs for a while," Dad said, concern lacing each word. He smiled, the skin crinkling at the corners of his eyes. "I wouldn't know what to do without my little girl."

I grabbed his hand and squeezed, my throat tightening. "Love you, Daddy."

"Love you too, kiddo."

The news anchor moved on to the next pile of shit, and I dug back into my salad.

"Who are you taking with you to the game on Sunday since I can't go?" Dad asked a few minutes later.

"I have a couple of people I could call."

"Just be careful and go straight home afterward," he suggested.

I nodded, having every intention of foregoing my usual barhopping downtown after games. "Promise, Daddy. So, what's the latest on that book of business you bid on last week?"

"I'm hoping to hear today. Zimmerman Insurance is a small entity, but they've been around for over fifty years."

He continued chatting, and my mind wandered to the unrelated Zimmerman haunting my dreams—while sleeping and awake. I hadn't gone out with anyone since him. Hadn't even logged into the three dating sites I used to find my sure-to-disappoint hookups.

Jessie had insisted I give Jarod a chance to break my shitty record, but I refused to bend. All the toys I kept in my bed stand had gotten a good workout over the last couple of weeks, but I'd been left unsatisfied and unable to get out of my depressive funk.

My life sucked ass, pure and simple.

Hot fudge, I thought, swallowing down my last bite of gag-worthy lunch. Over three scoops of moose tracks. Yeah, that would work to get me out of my head a little, but it would also slap another five pounds on my hips.

I snapped the lid on my empty container and pushed back my chair at the same time Dad did. Heading to my desk, I hoped no disgruntled customers walked through our door. Bitch mode was proving harder and harder to turn off.

My bad mood lasted throughout the day, all through

Saturday, and reached breaking point Sunday morning when I got a call from my friend who had agreed to go to the game with me.

She hacked up a lung while telling me she'd been running a fever for a few hours.

I heaved a sigh and glanced at the clock. It was eight in the morning with plenty of hours left before kickoff, but who the hell would be available last minute to use my extra ticket? The other handful of friends and acquaintances outside of work I'd contacted hadn't been available.

The two co-workers who loved football had plans, they told me when I reached out. Expecting another big fat no, I called Jessie who could care less about men smashing into each other on the gridiron.

"I'm sorry," she said, "but—"

"Come *on*," I all but whined. "Reid can stay with Cassie. Take a few hours for yourself and enjoy a girl's day out."

"She climbed into bed with us last night, and I hardly slept." I could make out the crack in Jessie's jaw—she must have yawned. "I can barely keep my eyes open, and it isn't even nine yet."

"Shit." I sighed, wracking my brain for who to call next. I was fresh out of friends worth poking.

"You could try Jarod," Jessie suggested, an all-too-obvious smile in her voice.

"Hardy-har." I pinched the bridge of my nose.

"I'm serious."

"I'll bet you are, but no."

"Well, whoever you decide to go with, just be sure to head home afterward and forego your usual barhopping."

"Yes, Mommy," I stated, sarcastic as hell.

Jessie laughed, and a few minutes later I hung up, gaze

glued to my cell's screen. Oh, the temptation…but calling Jarod wasn't an option since I didn't have his number.

My text notification dinged.

J: **Just in case…**

She included Jarod's contact info.

"Damn you." I dropped my phone onto the bed beside me and stared across my bedroom, unseeing. I didn't want to get involved with someone I liked too much to hurt. Yet I also couldn't get him out of my mind and move on with my pathetic life.

I snorted. I barely had one outside our family business. Sure, I had Dad and a couple of close friends, but lately, I'd felt like an aimless boat adrift at sea. No destination. No purpose outside passing the hours away. There was nothing driving me forward, no goals.

No dreams to fulfill.

But I had daydreams aplenty.

My throat tightened over a sense of loss I couldn't pinpoint or name. Something akin to…grief welled up inside me.

I picked up my phone, my hand suddenly shaking.

C: **Last minute, but want to go to the Pats game with me? This is Christine, btw. Jessie gave me your number.**

The inside of my lower lip fought with my teeth while I waited. Would he even answer? Tell me to fuck off? Agree with the excitement of a pubescent teen finally getting the girl? Or had he forgotten all about me in the plethora of pussy he'd been banging for Elite?

Heat welled up inside me and not the good kind. Just the thought of another woman on Jarod's body made me want to slice a bitch.

"The fuck is wrong with me?" I muttered, rubbing a hand over my face. Jealousy over a man I told myself I didn't want...

My cell dinged, giving me a single-worded response.

Sure.

I frowned even though my heart leapt. What the hell kind of answer was that? Hating the lack of tell through texting, I called rather than typing out some snarky shit that would probably make him change his mind.

Guess I was desperate or something. Blowing out a heavy exhale, I realized I *was*—but not just for company at the game.

"Christine," he answered.

"Don't sound so enthused," I said rather than greet him. I sounded like a petulant brat, but what else was new?

He chuckled. "If I'd have thrown a bunch of googley-eyed emojis and hearts back at you, you'd probably have texted back to forget you'd asked."

"You're probably right," I agreed although the idea of excitement in his reply fluttered my belly.

"Well then, *sure* it is."

"Okay." I hated that I grinned. Hated that my heart and panties melted at the sound of his voice over the phone. I would need to give one of my vibrators a workout before heading to Gillette.

"Want me to pick you up and drive us down there?" he asked.

"Sure," I sassed with a mocking tone, still smiling like a cupid-shot idiot.

Jarod outright laughed.

Chapter 24

Jarod

I couldn't keep my hand from shaking as I knocked on Christine's door. I'd debated on simply texting to let her know I'd pulled into her building's parking lot, but that felt too impersonal. The way she'd sounded on the phone, her invite alone, caused my head to spin.

Why ask me of all people to go to the game? Why reach out after walking out on me as though our night together had been nothing but an impersonal hookup? Why think of me at all unless she'd been just as haunted by the memories of our time together too?

Hope had me on a high, and while I'd hated canceling our guy's get-together at my place for the day's games, I'd done it without hesitation.

Cooney, Sean, and Micah had all wished me luck. They'd seen firsthand what Christine's breaking my heart had done to me.

Her door pulled inward before my thoughts went any further. She wore a blue Pats pullover sweatshirt and tight jeans that hugged her curves in all the right places.

Shoving my hands in my pockets, I stepped back rather

than pulling her into my arms. She'd sounded wary on the phone, and I wasn't about to push my luck. "Ready to go?"

"Yep." She turned and slid her key into the deadbolt, her shaking hands stilling my insides a little bit. Christine nervous *had* to be a good thing.

"Thanks for the invite," I said as she locked her house up. "It's been two years since I've gone to a game."

"I'm just glad I didn't have to go alone."

I cringed at her bored tone. "At least I made it on your to-call list—even if I was the last resort."

"Look." She stopped at the bottom of her stoop's stairs and turned, that chin of hers lifted. "I like you. A *lot*, but I'm not doing a relationship. I suck at them and don't want to break anyone's heart. We have some things in common and get along well enough, so let's just keep it at that, okay?"

Her eyes lied. She felt the energy radiating between us, that draw toward something bigger. Better than friendship and mere fucking.

"Okay," I agreed, amicable as shit and thoroughly chuffed inside.

She opened her mouth but snapped it shut as though surprised by my easy response. "Just like that?"

I made sure my gaze made my intentions known as I descended the stairs to stand beside her. I was all in. Ready to go to war since she'd given me an in. "Just like that."

Her lips pressed tight, and she hummed as though trying to figure my mind out.

A car's horn sounded up the street, seeming to pull her back to the present. "Fine, but none of those emotional I'm-crazy-about-you gazes shit. I can't handle it."

Rocking on my heels, hands still thoroughly buried in my pockets, I elbowed her arm. "How about I-want-to-fuck-you stares? Can you handle those instead?"

Her breath caught as our eyes met and held. "Barely."

I stared at her flushed face, imagining my lips on hers, my body pressed against her curves.

"I'll try to hide what you stir up inside me, Christine," I finally said, my gaze slipping down to the pulse throbbing in her neck, "but I can't help wanting you. I *can* promise to keep my hands to myself though. Deal?"

She nodded, her chest rising on a sharp inhale. "Deal."

I nodded toward my car waiting at the end of her walkway. "Then let's go enjoy the game."

"So." She stepped away from me, voice breezy as though determined to lighten the sexually charged atmosphere between us. I followed on her heels like a horny dog. "I'm dying to know what Micah had to say after our little exhibition the other week."

I bit back a groan while pulling out my car keys. "You really want to discuss sex with me right now?" I asked, keeping my voice low as she drew up beside my car.

"Did he tell you that he offered me a job?" She angled toward me, the warm sun glinting fire in her hair.

A muscle ticked in my jaw as I made sense of her question. The resulting possessive flare of jealousy heated me through—and not in a good way.

Christine raised an eyebrow.

"No." I clipped the word.

Her lips twitched. "Just kidding."

Cursing, I stabbed the unlock button on my key fob. "You're going to be the death of me," I muttered.

I opened the passenger door, but she hesitated from climbing in, the small space between us was way too much for my liking. Those green eyes of hers peered into mine, reaching inside me and twisting my insides up tight.

As if the woman didn't already have a clenching grip on my soul as it was.

"I don't think I'd like a world without Jarod Zimmerman in it," she whispered as though an epiphany had come to light inside her head.

Talk about fucking hope. It exploded like fireworks inside my chest, brightening every cell inside my body.

I held her stare so she would see my determination and understand the lengths I would go to in order to win the war over her fears. I'd already conquered mine—hell, *she* had done that without trying—and I looked forward to watching hers crumble. "You've just given me a reason to be even more ambitious."

She huffed. "Don't get any ideas."

"Too late." I grinned and nodded toward the passenger seat. "Sit your fine ass down, woman. We've got a football game and beer awaiting us."

Keeping things on a friend level was torture for my cock but totally doable since her words and body language spoke for themselves. She wanted me. Her dilated pupils and heightened pulse jumping in her neck every time our bodies brushed against each other only confirmed my assumptions.

I kept the conversation light, and we didn't lack things to talk about. Sure, we had only spent a total of two nights together, but I swore we'd known each other for years. We'd connected in ways far beyond our shared love of sports and hops with an ease that seemed too effortless. Scary as fuck and yet oh so right. But how could I make her see the truth of what we could be before she fled?

I focused on taking in the sights of Gillette and the outrageously expensive food and drinks rather than staring at her expressive face. I focused on the Pats crushing the Texans instead of how she screamed and cursed, jumping to her feet in either excitement or pissiness over a bullshit call. I focused on the long walk back to my car amidst thousands of other fans heading off to celebrate our win when all I wanted to do was drag her against my side and tuck her in close for safe keeping.

Our boys had crushed their opponents, continuing their winning streak and giving us confidence they would go on to win the AFC Championship. Both of us exited the stadium on a high, our feet light even as we traipsed down the road toward the self-storage business we'd parked at.

As with throughout the game, we discussed calls, the ways our defense had ruled the field, and our offense dominated. Neither of us mentioned Jackson or the fact he'd been on the field for the first time since his injury. He'd played a good game though. I had to give him that.

But he wasn't the man who got to take Christine home.

"Where to?" I asked once I sat behind the wheel, my nose and fingertips slightly chilled from the brisk fall evening.

Christine shrugged, her lower lip sucking in between her teeth. Our gazes held over the console, filling me with an ache I saw echoed in her eyes.

"You're ready to call it a night, but you're *not* ready to call it a night," I said. "Does that nonsense about sum it up?"

She wrinkled her nose. "Am I that obvious?"

"No less than me."

She laughed lightly, turning away to put on her seat belt. "What a pair we make, huh?"

Fuck yeah, we did. I caught her gaze and smiled, wanting her and yet completely content to even just sit beside her for another hour. "So. How about a drink?"

"Depends where."

"While I'd love to say my place or yours—" I waggled

my eyebrows "—I'm thinking O'Neill's." A safer choice for her, one she'd be more inclined to agree to so our time together wouldn't end.

She hesitated a few seconds, and I let her figure out what she wanted while I made my way out of the parking lot.

"I promised my dad and Jessie I would avoid Boston bars," she finally said, "but O'Neill's isn't a huge dance joint. It ought to be safe enough."

It took a long, fucking time, but we finally headed north toward the city. Same as our ride to Gillette Stadium, the conversation didn't wane. A comfortable companionship filled my car, regardless of the sexual energy beneath the surface tempting me to push for more.

We claimed a small table in the back of my favorite bar forty-five minutes later. A nice dim corner tucked against the brick wall to hide away from the busy bar and kitchen so we could chat over the din of happy Pats fans and the hint of music beneath. The hallway leading to the bathrooms lay to my right, giving us extra privacy and me the chance to face the other patrons and better keep an eye on shit.

Nothing worse than having to sit with your back to a room.

A cold bottle of beer between my hands, I studied the woman across from me whose gaze flitted around the bar. "Is your date boring you?" I asked, hating the flare of jealousy when her eyes lingered on a buff guy in too tight of a T-shirt checking her out.

"Nope." She swigged from her bottle and turned back toward me, giving me her undivided attention. I stared at her lips as they peeled off the rim, moist and lush. "But this isn't a *date*."

"Call it whatever you want," I said with a grin, loving

how she'd dismissed the guy, "but I've gotten to hang with you longer than most men you kick to the curb."

"True." She sipped again, her green eyes peering into mine as though reading my mind.

Rather than leaving her to guess, I leaned forward, elbows on the table. "Why?"

She rolled her eyes and took a long drink of her beer. "You're annoying as hell," she muttered, but no annoyance showed on her face.

"*Why*, Christine?" I pushed for an answer, wanting some truth laid out in the space between us, something to help me bridge the gap and grant me access behind her walls.

A heavy exhale left her, her lips thinning as she studied me.

I refused to sit back and let it go.

"Because you intrigue me," she finally confessed, her tone unhappy. "You also scare the shit out of me."

I grinned over finally getting a peek behind enemy lines in our war I had every intention of winning. "I like the sound of that."

"I don't." Christine sat back on her chair, her gaze roaming over my face, shoulders, and chest, coming to rest on my hands wrapped around my beer. "You're a great guy..."

"Here comes the but."

She smiled. "Actually, I was going to say *and*, as in and any woman would be lucky to have you."

"But?" I supplied since I knew the word rested in her wary mind.

"I'm not her."

"You could be."

Her mouth opened, but she shut it again, shaking her

head. She picked at the bottle's label with a fingernail. "I would end up breaking your heart like I have every other guy who has fallen for me."

"Awfully confident of that fact, aren't you?"

"I've left enough broken hearts in my wake to know it's the truth."

I pushed my beer off to the side and leaned forward, crossing my arms on the table. She'd given a bullshit reason, but I could focus on the real one keeping her from agreeing to what we both longed for. "What if I'm willing to risk it all?"

Christine lifted her head and stared at me. "Why would you do that?"

"Because you intrigue *me*. You also scare the shit out of me."

Chuckling, she raised her bottle in mock cheers and sucked down a few swallows.

"Because I also think you're worth it," I continued, refusing to lighten the mood like she seemed to desperately want to do. "I love your confidence. Your drive."

"You also love my ass," she stated, placing her bottle back on the table.

"More than you could imagine." All trace of a smile faded from my lips and eyes. "You're the first and only woman who has made me think about more than just emptying my balls, Christine. You know about my parents, why I've been dead set against any sort of relationship."

She eyed me over the table, nodding slowly.

"But you make me believe the good times could outweigh the bad," I murmured, putting every ounce of emotion I felt into my words. "That the minutes, the hours or days of bliss we could find together would be worth any possible future heartache."

Christine sucked in a breath as though I'd touched a tender part inside her. Her eyes welled. "Jarod—"

Voices raised harshly from the entrance, and I shifted to see around Christine. The bouncer checking IDs by the door held onto a man's arm. Red-faced, the would-be patron in the bulky zipper-down tried to push his way inside. The bouncer grabbed hold of his sweatshirt and yanked, but the material gave way beneath their scuffle.

A shiver shot through me like a bullet, followed by a rush of adrenaline at the sight of the vest beneath the guy's sweatshirt.

"Shit!" I grabbed Christine's hand and yanked her from her seat, spinning for the hallway on our right. There wasn't an exit, but any space I could put between us and that guy...

A flash lit my periphery as I pulled Christine alongside me, and a whoosh of air blew me off my feet and farther into the hallway. Screams and a blast echoed in my ears as darkness descended, forcing me to the ground.

Chapter 25

Jarod

My heartbeat thudded in my ears as I blinked. Dust stung my eyes, and I coughed. "Christine?" I squeezed my hand to find her fingers still wrapped in mine. "Christine!"

I jolted upright but smashed my head. A wall of solid *something* hovered directly overhead—and to my right, I noted while reaching out in the pitch black.

"Fuck!" Shifting to my knees and keeping my head low, I moved closer to Christine. My free hand scrambled along her arm, up to her face. Wetness coated her cheek.

"Oh, fuck! Fuck!" I scooted in closer, blinking and trying to see her through the dense darkness surrounding us. Adrenaline shot through me. "Christine!"

She moaned.

"Oh, thank Christ! Are you okay?" I swallowed hard, my blood rushing through my system.

Another moan, this one louder, sounded from her, and she squeezed my hand.

"I'm right here."

Training kicking in, I pressed against her side, slowly

taking stock of what had happened while pressing two fingers against her neck. "You've got a good pulse. You're okay."

The guy had a bomb strapped to his fucking chest.

We were buried in rubble.

My chest went tight, my breathing going shallow regardless of my adrenaline gland pumping overtime.

Chill the fuck out, Zimmerman. You're alive. Make sure Christine is okay.

"Can you move?" I whispered, running my hand down over her body as far as I could reach, my entire body shaky as fuck. I encountered wetness on her thigh—and a massive piece of rubble resting on her left leg.

Shit, shit, shit!

I'd attempt to save her, and she ended up injured while I...a few aches made themselves known, but I was too amped up to feel the full effects of having been blasted from behind.

"I—I don't—" She coughed. "I think my nose got fucked up."

"Shh." Teeth clenched, I returned my hand up her body, gently running my fingertips over her face, desperately trying to slow my pounding heart. She definitely had a broken nose. I moved my touch around the other side of her face and up into her hair. A massive bump swelled above her temple, covered in wetness.

Head wounds always bled like a motherfucker, but that was a lot...

Cursing, I struggled to yank my sweatshirt off in the tight space we were trapped in, realizing in the movement that I had definitely fucked up my shoulder. Probably landed on it. I also had a broken index finger, I realized, as even more pain receptors came online in my brain.

I managed to untangle myself and turned my sweatshirt inside out. She didn't make a sound as I pressed the hopefully clean area of the material against the side of her head.

"What happened?" she murmured.

"Bomb."

"Are we dead?" she asked in a deadpan voice as though she didn't care one way or the other.

"No." I tried to peer through the darkness for any hint of light but couldn't see a goddamned thing. The adrenaline began to wear off, bumps and bruises making themselves known in sharper focus.

Cell phone...I'd left mine on the table beside my beer. "Where's your cell?" I asked, not remembering if Christine had a purse...no, she hadn't. "Christine?" I nudged her when she didn't answer. "Hey...stay awake," I encouraged since I had no fucking clue how hard she'd hit her head.

"M'kay."

I released a heavy exhale at the sound of her voice in the stillness suffocating us. "Do you have your cell on you?"

She shifted—and whimpered.

"Shh. It's okay. Don't try to shift around too much."

"Back...pocket."

The damn thing had probably shattered from how she'd landed face-up, but it was worth a shot if I could get to it.

"I'm gonna try to get your cell—I don't want you to move though. Just lay still while I feel around for it."

Christine didn't make a single joke as I fished my hand without the broken finger beneath her lower back, groping along her ass.

Bingo.

I shifted the phone free from her pocket, wiggled it from beneath the weight of her body, and tapped the screen.

The sudden light stung my eyes like a gunshot to my

brain, but I exhaled in relief that the thing even worked. The screen a shattered mess, it refused to read her face to unlock and let me call 911. Or maybe the facial ID didn't recognize her beneath all the dirt and blood...fuck, I'd have to check a bit closer once I got someone on the phone. Eyes closed and lips parted, she appeared too damn still. "What's your pin?"

Christine didn't answer, and I poked her side. Her brow furrowed, but she didn't lift her eyelids. "Hmm?"

"Pin—what's your cell phone pin?"

She whispered out the six digits, and I tapped the first number with my ring finger—nothing.

"Shit," I muttered, trying again, but the screen refused to acknowledge my touch other than to keep the screen lit. "Goddamnit."

The light blinked out, leaving us once more in darkness. Swiping it back on, I held it over Christine's filthy face, taking in the damage. A deep laceration bit into her scalp above the massive bump but not severe enough that she would bleed to death. I could only guess how bad of a concussion she had.

"Can you open your eyes for me?" I asked, needing to see her pupils.

She blinked—winced. "Ow."

"I know," I murmured, rubbing my thumb over the one cheekbone not beat to hell. "Let me see those gorgeous emerald eyes, Christine. Please."

Another blink allowed me a quick glance to see her pupils were the same size.

"Good girl," I whispered as her eyelids fluttered shut once more.

Blood smeared beneath her crooked nose, and I thinned my lips, taking in the rest of the scratches over her face.

Christine looked like she'd spent ten rounds in a boxing ring. I felt the same but couldn't be bothered with my own pains since nothing seemed life-threatening.

Another swipe to keep the screen alive, and I angled the light down over the rest of her body.

One pile of rubble enclosing us in our tiny hole lay atop her right leg, and the blood on her left thigh had me shifting in the tight space to check it over.

A few cuts, one that would need stitches, but again, not enough to make her bleed out.

I pulled off my shirt and attempted to tie it tight around her thigh, my awkwardly bent finger hindering my ability to create a knot.

Christine didn't make a sound.

"Hey." I took her left, limp hand in mine, scanning over her slack face. "Christine."

"Hmm?" She roused enough to flutter her fingers against mine.

"You probably have a concussion. I need you to stay awake for me, okay?"

"Don't wanna." Her slurred words barely reached my ears in the stifling space around us.

I let the cell's screen go dark, saving it since I had no clue how long we would be trapped. "Talk to me."

"'Bout what?" She sighed.

"The weather. Your favorite way to eat lobster. Anything." I lay down beside her, the floor covered in dirt and bits of who the fuck knew what pressing into my bare skin. At least it wasn't cold in our little tomb.

"You said...you said I was your best," she whispered with hardly any tone to her voice.

A fucking ice pick stabbed into my heart at the memory

of her walking away from me what seemed forever ago. "Yes."

"D-did you mean it?"

I caressed the back of her hand with my thumb. "Every fucking word."

Christine sighed. "I should have...should have given us a shot while I had the chance."

"You still can." I pressed in closer, wrapping my free arm over her but taking care to not jostle her body. The longer she lay in shock, unaware of how badly she'd been injured, the better.

"Wh-what if we don't make it out of here?" she asked in the darkness, hopelessness settled over her voice as heavy as the wreckage above us.

"We will. I promise."

I clenched my eyes shut and prayed harder than I ever had before.

Chapter 26

Christine

Jarod kept talking to me. His voice hurt my ears. I wanted to sleep, but the bastard wouldn't let me. He couldn't just drone on about his childhood...no. Every other sentence out of his mouth was a question, and if I didn't answer him right away, he would jab me with one of the fingers I clasped against my side.

My left leg began to hurt. Head throbbed. I'd never known such thirst. My throat scratched from breathing in dust.

I wanted to sleep. Couldn't open my eyes whenever he asked me to.

"Your head stopped bleeding."

"Mmm," I voiced acknowledgment of having heard him so he wouldn't poke me again.

His hand caressed my cheek and my chin before disappearing. Clicking sounded a few times through the ringing in my ears.

"Whas that?" I tried asking but had difficulty forming the words past the fuzziness in my head.

"I'm tapping SOS with my watch against whatever this slab of rubble is overhead. Some sort of metal."

"M'kay."

The deliberate sound happened again, rousing me from the haziness creeping over my brain.

"Want to play a game?" he asked and clicked again.

"Uh huh." I tried to swallow the dryness from my throat. Water would be nice. A cold brew even better.

So damn tired.

"Rapid-fire interview. Ready?"

"Shh," I said as Jarod clicked out the SOS again, the tap, tap, tapping more like a gong going off between my ears. Wincing only made my nose hurt even worse.

"Favorite color?" he asked, his breath fanning my cheek.

I started to fade into oblivion, lured by the lessened pain of unconsciousness.

A sharp jab in my side jolted me back to awareness, and I blinked in the darkness.

"Favorite color," Jarod repeated.

"Blue," I answered, my eyelids fluttering closed once more. *So fucking thirsty!*

The damn noise again, an annoying, persistent jab in my brain.

"Favorite season?"

"Football," I murmured my easy answer he already knew.

Jarod laughed. "Of course it is."

I smiled which stung my nose like a bitch. "Nose hurts."

"How's your leg?" he asked before another SOS echoed in my ears.

I took stock of where my legs ought to be, where the pain had been rippling upward toward my core what seemed hours before. Couldn't reach down to feel them though. Didn't have the energy. Just wanted to sleep...

"Hey..."

"Hmm?"

"How's your right leg?"

"Can't really feel it," I murmured, drifting toward the horizon of oblivion.

"Can you wiggle your toes on either side?" Jarod's question once more tugged me back to reality.

I tried to do as he'd asked but couldn't really tell if any of them moved or not. "Don't know, Nurse Zimmerman."

He chuckled and sent another SOS. "What's the best advantage to being tall?" he asked, and I had to think...make sense of his question. Once I did, I answered the first thing that came to mind.

"I fit perfectly against you. Beneath you." I sighed at the sweet memory of his skin against mine. All hot and hard. Strong. Safe. I tightened my hold on his hand.

Jarod cursed near my ear, keeping me with him. "The best thing you've ever done?"

"You." There was no point in lying to him—or myself. Our time was running out, and I found myself regretting the choices I'd made to keep him at arm's length. My eyes stung as the reality of where we were and what had happened settled down over me.

We'd been buried alive...in a small space. How long until our air got used up? What happened when rescuers began climbing atop the rubble and shifted the walls, and beams rained down atop us? O'Neill's used to be a three-story building...and who knew how much separated us from ever seeing the light of day again.

"Number one complaint?" Jarod's next question

maneuvered my mind from a path sure to lead to panic and losing my shit.

I grasped at his hand, assuring myself he still lay beside me. Pebbles...something bit into my back, but I couldn't even shift to make myself more comfortable. The hard floor beneath my head offered no softness, nor did the area beneath my shoulder blades.

So uncomfortable. Thirsty.

Tired.

"Number one complaint," Jarod repeated, pulling my hazed brain back into focus.

"I shouldn't have walked out on you," I whispered, my voice reedy thin, sounding as broken as my body.

Jarod kissed the side of my head before clicking another SOS on that damn bit of metal he'd managed to find. "You're going to get another chance to stay, even if I have to dig our way out of here."

I tried to squeeze his hand tighter, desperate to hang onto him regardless of the fuzziness slipping over my mind again. "Don't leave me."

"I won't." More damn clicking jolted through me.

Dad...

My throat tightened. I'd done what I'd promised I wouldn't—gone to a bar after the game. Nothing good ever came from disobeying my daddy. I thought I'd learned that as a teenager, but I guess not—

"Greatest fear?"

I considered Jarod's question, taking a few seconds to process it since thoughts of never seeing my father again battled for dominance over my emotions. Attempting light-hearted, I said, "Not being stuck in small places, thank God."

His quiet chuckle ghosted warm breath over my cheek, and a tear trickled from beneath my eyelids.

I wanted to snuggle in closer to Jarod, an instinct to hide against him, close my eyes, and escape reality for a while. *This man...*

He had deserved more of me. My effort in finding a way to open my heart to love. I'd never wanted it before him. Never had allowed myself to dream.

And now I had no time left to show him the level of affection I'd stifled.

Did I sleep?

I blinked in the darkness, noting that Jarod gently touched my face.

"Still with me?" he whispered, his voice ragged as though as parched and tired as I was.

"Mmm," I hummed, once more murky between the ears.

The clinking SOS clashed against my brain. Goddamn him...no. He was trying to let rescuers know where we were...

"Greatest fear?" he asked again.

"Grizzlies," I answered without thought. I'd had enough nightmares of them as a kid even though I'd never seen one in real life.

"I won't ever take you to Yellowstone or Alaska," Jarod said, his voice as soothing as aloe on a sunburn.

"Yours?" I asked, fighting for every last second I had with the man who I wished I'd allowed myself to love. It would have been better to enjoy him in the moments we'd had even though it had been short.

It would have been worth it.

He would have been worth it.

"Used to be dying, but I've found something else that I

fear more," Jarod answered, keeping me from spiraling into tears.

"Whas that?" I murmured, my voice sounding like no more than a drunken slur even though I'd only had a couple of beers throughout the entire day.

"Dying without having a chance to tell you how I feel about you."

Butterflies took to flight in my stomach, and my breath caught regardless of the heaviness of darkness beckoning me to slip away again. "So tell me," I whispered, an emotional basket case on the verge of losing my sanity.

"I'm well and truly fucked, Christine."

A barked laugh tried to rip from my lungs at the resignation in his tone, but I started to cough. Fucking pain tore through me from head to toes I could *definitely* feel.

"Shh." He soothed me, hands soft on my breast.

"P-pretty sure *I'm* the one who got fucked that night," I rasped out once I caught my breath.

"If you weren't in pain and trapped beneath whatever the fuck is on top of your leg, I'd find a way inside your pants right now." His voice teased, but I expected he really would have if given the chance.

Warmth spread through me, and even though our situation sucked donkey ass, I knew I would have let him. Begged for it even. I floated in the comfort of his nearness, the contentment of darkness. Carefree. No thoughts.

A poke jabbed in my side. "Christine?"

"Hmm?" My hum echoed in my ears.

"Stay with me, sweet girl."

"M'kay."

The clicking sounded and ended as the blackness took me completely.

Chapter 27

Jarod

We'd been buried for six hours according to Christine's cell phone. I'd tried to use the light sparingly, only swiping it to life if she whimpered or I felt compelled to check her wounds. Both her head and thigh had stopped bleeding, but I couldn't keep her conscious for very long periods of time.

At least she sounded decently coherent when awake, answering me with full sentences.

I wasted a few minutes of her cell's battery using the lit screen to fully check out our tomb. I'd been lucky to not have any parts of my body crushed beneath the wood, metal, and crumbling sheetrock piled around us, but I definitely hadn't escaped unscathed. My shoulder was dislocated, my index finger definitely cracked, and my knee throbbed. Nothing felt broken around my kneecap, but I must have twisted my leg while going down. Once on my feet—*when* we got out of there—I'd be better able to assess that situation.

There was no hint of light through the rubble, nothing to give me hope I could somehow crawl out and drag her along with me though. We lay at the mercy of the crews sure to sift through the mess around us.

At least our table had been against an exterior wall, as had the hallway I'd headed toward when I realized what had been about to happen. With two floors overhead, I expected we still had plenty of rubble atop us, but better our location there than in the thick of the bar's middle though.

Christine's leg lay crushed by a beam, one I wouldn't be able to budge even if I wanted to attempt digging us free—which I didn't. The last fucking thing I needed was for the pressure to release from whatever injury lay beneath.

I expected our air to run out, but with every passing hour, that fear lessened. As long as the bomb's debris overhead didn't shift and completely bury us, we could live a couple of days without water. I'd heard of countless people being pulled from the wreckage of fallen buildings long after they shouldn't have.

What choice did I have but to hold onto the hope the click of my watch on the metal above my head would eventually be heard?

Initially, Christine had winced every time I tapped, but she'd fallen past the point of being annoyed by the only noise inside our claustrophobic pocket of space. She might not be bothered by small enclosures, but I sure as fuck was.

Once back in grade school, our class had taken a trip to some underground caverns. The stalactites had been cool as shit, but the cold darkness that had pressed against me on all sides when they'd turned out the lights to let us experience the feeling of being buried alive?

Fucking hell.

I'd almost peed my damn pants. More than one kid had

cried, but I'd managed to swipe my tears away without making a sound.

Catching hints of honeysuckle helped keep my brain focused on what mattered most. The softness of Christine's limp hand in mine with the occasional gentle squeeze of her fingers gave me something else to keep my brain from flipping the fuck out throughout the night. Eventually, I grew accustomed to the stifling atmosphere around us, or perhaps exhaustion had finally won me over.

I startled awake, blinking in the pitch black.

We were still buried.

"Fuck." I rubbed a hand over my face and realized I'd dropped the cell phone. Feeling around in the darkness, I located it on the other side of Christine where I'd had my arm draped.

A swipe lit the sad truth of our situation.

"Christine?" I murmured, shifting onto my elbow so I could see her face better. "Hey." I released her hand and gently prodded her side like I'd done countless times in the first couple of hours.

She didn't respond. Didn't move.

"Christine," I stated louder, shaking her enough to rouse any slumbering person. Still, she didn't react. "Fuck." I checked her pulse—steady although weaker than I'd have liked.

Scrambling onto my knees, I gently lifted one of her eyelids.

She was out cold.

"Goddamnit!" I choked back a sob, glancing around at the wreckage pressing closer against me.

No...

"Oh fuck." I gulped, fighting to still my racing heart. The light went off, and I clenched my eyes shut, counting on inhales. Counting out exhales. Slow and steady, talking myself out of a panic attack. I had to keep my sanity.

SOS—I tapped overhead, gulping for air, hunger and thirst adding a desperate measure of need to my instinct to *live.*

I'd promised Christine I would get us out of there. Free us, give us a chance to pursue what both of us had been too scared to explore.

I wanted to love her, goddamnit! Wanted to hold her while she slept every night. Wanted to kiss her awake every morning.

Tears slid down my face, and I leaned over her in the darkness, needing to feel the softness of her lips, her exhale mingling with mine. The cushion of her mouth gave way beneath mine, unmoving yet warm. I lingered there, soaking in the knowledge her heart still pumped, and her lungs still worked to give oxygen to her broken body.

"We *will* escape this hell hole," I whispered as more tears dripped from my face. "And I'm going to love you so damn hard. No holding back. No regrets allowed for either of us."

A muffled holler sounded in the distance—or perhaps mere feet away.

"Hey!" I screamed back. "We're here!"

Silence followed for a few of my frantic-paced heartbeats.

"Hello!" the voice came again.

"We're here!" I yelled as loud as I could, wincing at the echo of my shriek. I fumbled with the cell, lighting the screen and shining it upward, flashing it overhead on the roof right above me. "Down here!"

Dust rained over on my head, and I shied away, glancing quickly over at Christine.

She still lay unmoved, unfazed by my hollering.

Blinking in the motes of particles in the air, I called a few times, and someone replied almost immediately.

They heard me. Had to have—I just couldn't make out clearly what they said.

I flashed the light around until the battery died, leaving us in darkness once more. Maybe they'd caught a glimpse of it through the cracks of our prison.

"They're coming for us," I told Christine, gently touching her face, not sure if she could hear or even understand me. She hadn't even flinched at the ruckus. "Hang in there." I kissed her lips again, allowing myself to fully hope we would have a future. Together.

God knew we would both probably end up with a bad case of PTSD, and I would definitely have even worse claustrophobic issues than I did as a kid, but at least I would get to experience it. Remember I'd survived. Have the chance to love when I never thought a relationship would be in my cards.

I wanted that. Phobias and all. Would gladly welcome them if it mean loving on Christine for the rest of our lives.

The muffled voice grew louder—another joined in. Soon, I could hear the sounds of movement, shifting weight toward our left. One loud thump and grit wafted into my eyes. I closed them for a time, yelling on occasion when the guys checked in with me.

It seemed hours, but I could clearly hear voices—they asked our names. I gave them, the state of Christine, and they promised to get us out soon. EMTs were on hand to take care of my woman.

She would be just fine.

Cool air slid over my face, and I squinted in the dust.

Light flickered through some of the debris.

"I can see you!" I hollered, my voice breaking on a sob. "I see you!"

"We got them!" A guy yelled, a stab of light flashing directly on my face through bent metal and splintered wood.

Tears coursed down my cheeks, and I hovered over Christine, gently wrapping her in my arms and shielding her in case anything fell atop us in the rescuers' attempts to dig us free. They'd actually found us...more tears poured even though I felt dehydrated as hell. While I wasn't fond of needles, I couldn't *wait* to be hooked up to an IV—

A hand touched my shoulder. "Jarod."

Turning, I took in the face of a stranger, a man covered in filth like me, his hard hat askew. His grin proved contagious. "Everything's going to be okay," he said.

I glanced down at Christine—she still lay pale and unmoving beneath the early morning light filtering in through the tangled mess around us. "I'm gonna love you forever, sweet girl."

Chapter 28

Christine

Pain shot down through my leg, and I came awake with a shriek, thrashing. "Fuck!" I screamed again, agony radiating up my thigh and blinding lights killing my eyes.

"The hell are you doing to her?" I heard Jarod holler from too far away.

I closed my right hand into a fist, but his fingers weren't there for me to grasp.

"Jarod!" Blinking and squinting, I could barely make out the man leaning over me.

"Shh," he soothed with his voice as pressure once more as coolness slid through my body, numbing the pain and easing my mind. "We're getting you out of here."

"Need him..."

"He'll come along with us to the hospital."

I closed my eyes and gave over to the darkness again, trusting Jarod to be there when I woke again.

ℋℰ

A warm hand slid down my cheek, and I breathed in deeply, my mind swimming through a murky haze. At least there was no pain.

"Hey, sweetheart."

"Daddy," I murmured, smiling at the voice I'd know anywhere.

"Thank God." Dad's voice broke, and I recognized the strong fingers squeezing my left hand.

I forced my eyelids open. Dim light bathed the fuzziness around me. No more dust stung my nose, nor did choking dryness scratch my throat. I floated in a painless wave that didn't quite feel real, but I could grasp Dad's hand. Could smell the scent of his cologne I'd adored since childhood.

"I'm alive," I whispered even though I didn't have the energy to pinch myself just to be sure.

"Yes," Dad said, his voice wobbling. "You're at Mass General."

I turned my head slowly, searching the small hospital room as it gradually came into focus. "Where's Jarod?"

"I sent him home to shower and change out of the borrowed scrubs he's been wearing since they brought you both here."

"He's okay?"

"Banged up a bit. A broken finger is the worst of his injuries."

It took me some time to process his answer, but I turned my head back toward Dad. "How long?"

"Three days since the explosion, two since you were admitted." Wetness welled in his eyes, and he lifted my hand, kissing my knuckles.

"I'm sorry," I murmured, my voice sounding tired as the rest of me felt.

"You have nothing to be sorry about."

"I promised I wouldn't go any bars downtown, but I didn't want our night to end and neither of our places would have been safe." It took me awhile to get all the words out, but Dad didn't interrupt.

He stared at me as though working through my explanation. "You love him," he finally stated as though certain.

"I-I'm not sure?" I'd never felt that kind of emotion before, had only seen it with him and Mom.

A flicker of sorrow slithered through my chest at the memory of her same as it always did, but thoughts of Jarod, of how much I longed for him, overshadowed the hurt.

"Maybe," I amended my answer, but that didn't feel quite right either. "Want him. Need him."

Dad's slow smile and the welling of more tears shouldn't have made me happy. "Take it from a man who had been blessed with two decades of being with my soulmate—you *do* love that boy, and I couldn't be happier."

I owed Jarod my life, and even more importantly, I did want him to share in whatever days I had left. Better to have loved and lost...

I finally understood what Dad had meant when talking about Mom.

"You better like him," I whispered, peering over at my dad with as much seriousness as I could muster, "because I'm not pushing this one away."

"He seems like a nice young man," Dad said, lifting a water bottle with a built-in straw to my lips. "He was by your side when I got here, and if it weren't for my insisting he go home and clean up, would probably still be sitting here holding your hand."

Ice water slid down my parched throat, and I smacked

my lips, humming over its deliciousness. "How bad is my leg?" I asked as Dad set the water on the table beside him.

"It's pretty banged up but will be fine. They had taken you straight into surgery. If that broken wall hadn't trapped your thigh, you would have bled out," he said, tucking some of my hair behind my ear.

"Shit."

"You might need another surgery, but at least they gave us assurance you won't lose your leg."

"I'm breathing—that's all that matters."

Dad made a noise of agreement. "The doctor said you'll be on morphine for another day or two, but once you're discharged, they'll put you on something milder so you won't be so loopy."

It felt like a good buzz, numb teeth and lips included. Better than the few seconds of sheer agony I'd experienced while being pulled from the rubble.

"When can I get back to work? Can I still go to next week's game?"

Dad chuckled. "One day at a time, kiddo."

"M'kay." A sigh shuddered down my body.

"Cold?" he asked, tugging a bleach-scented blanket up beneath my chin.

"No."

"Why don't you rest now, sweetheart," Dad said and kissed my forehead. "I'm going to head home for the night and come back in the morning."

"G'night," I managed before morphine-induced sleep rolled over my brain, tugging me into a darkness I didn't need to fear.

ℲE

Warmth encased my right side. Citrus and spice filled my nose, hot breath fanned my cheek.

I opened my eyes and turned my head slightly to take in the man tucked into the narrow hospital bed beside me. Bed rails kept us plastered together.

A scratch lined Jarod's bruised cheekbone above a couple of days' worth of scruff, but I'd never seen anyone so damn fine in all my life.

"Hey," I said, tingles racing through my blood and waking my brain and body more than it had been in...hours? Days?

He smiled, erasing the tiredness from his eyes even though dark circles lay beneath them. "Hey back," he murmured, brushing his knuckles over my cheek.

"You okay?" I asked.

"My entire body hurts but nothing serious," he replied.

I smoothed back his mussed hair with a hand stuck by an IV line and covered in tape. Even exhausted, Jarod was hella hot. Beautiful—heart-achingly so. How...why had I denied the connection between us? I'd been given a second chance to live life to the fullest, and I wasn't going to waste another second.

"I'm sure I've got two black eyes from my broken nose and my breath probably reeks," I whispered, "but I would really love if you'd kiss me right now."

Jarod pressed his lips softly against mine, and I sighed, melting into a puddle of contentment.

He pulled back way too soon and threaded his fingers through mine, resting our hands on my chest. "I don't think I ever told you how I feel about you," he said, peering down at me.

I bit back a smirk, remembering some of what he'd

shared with me while we'd been buried alive. "Meaning you're more than fucked?"

"Meaning I'm falling in love with you, Christine Gemberling."

God. There it was out in the open between us. The "L" word.

I stared at him, my chest tight even though my heart felt like it flew through bright sunshine. "Is there a cure for such a thing, Nurse Zimmerman?" I asked rather than replying with the canned response most people would expect—what I realized was absolute truth with having Jarod all up in my space again.

"Sure as hell hope there isn't," Jarod murmured, his thumb rubbing over my lower lip.

"Then I guess we're doomed."

His slow smirk heated me regardless of the morphine attempting to numb the cells in my body.

"So." I shifted to relieve the sweet ache between my thighs, pressing a leg against his groin. "When I get out of here, want to play doctor for real?"

His huff of laughter shook my hospital bed. "I'll play whatever the hell you want if it means hanging around long after you'd usually kick a guy to the curb."

"I can live with that," I said and lifted my head to kiss him again.

Chapter 29

Jarod

My finger, sprained knee, and shoulder healed long before Christine's leg. She'd been through two surgeries to fix the damage to her upper thigh and its shattered bone, and she'd been lucky the rest of her leg had completely escaped injury in the pocket beyond the beam that had held her down and kept her from bleeding out.

I sat in the waiting room while she worked with her physical therapist, my thoughts scrolling through the weeks since the explosion that had toppled the building around us. Nightmares occasionally haunted both of us, but waking in the other's arms brought the solace we needed.

We hadn't officially moved in together, but I spent more time at her place than I did my own, sleeping beside her warmth every night since I couldn't bear to be away from her when the lights went out.

Oftentimes, we fell asleep with our hands clasped. We woke that way too with my body a protective shield wrapped around her. She had told me the night before that she never thought she would like having someone in her bed but now couldn't imagine sleeping without me.

I switched up my hours at the children's hospital, cutting back to four ten-hour shifts so I could spend the bulk of my time with Christine. Still on crutches, my woman hobbled around and definitely needed assistance with daily tasks. While she remained stubbornly independent, she allowed me to shower with her and pamper her in whatever way she required to be comfortable.

You *are my comfort*, she had told me the night before.

The memory of finally giving in to her begging for my cock slid through my blood like an infusion of heat.

Leaning forward, elbows on knees, I closed my eyes and relived slowly pressing into her slick warmth. Her body had welcomed me, wrapped around me the best she could with one healing thigh.

Becoming one with her after weeks of not being able to sink into her heaven had tripled the emotional tether between us. We had shared breaths, our mouths hungry and searching. Staring into her eyes while burying balls deep and giving her everything I had filled me with such potent feelings...

A shudder rippled down my spine, and I swallowed hard.

She'd come so damn hard around my dick, her pussy a pulsing vise that had made my balls detonate to the point I saw literal stars. Then she'd cradled my body in her softness when I sagged atop her.

I'd thought for sure I would get the *I love you* I'd been dying for in response to my declaration, but she teased the same as always, hinting at how she felt without actually saying it.

Stubborn brat.

Snickering, I shook my head and sat back, well aware I wouldn't want her any other way. A heavy inhale and slow release filled and emptied my lungs. I couldn't help the grin on my face. I could live without the words. Christine showed me with her actions and every lingering gaze exactly how much she loved me.

Things hadn't been perfect since the rescuers had pulled us from the wreckage of what had once been O'Neill's, but we'd meandered our way through, ending every argument with physical affection and words of thankfulness for our survival. Having the chance for another day with one another.

We'd been lucky—far more than over a dozen others hadn't survived the tragedy. Neither Christine nor I had personally known any of those who'd perished, but we'd visited the site a week after her release from the hospital. Dozens of flowers had piled along the chain-link fence surrounding the location, and we added those we'd brought to honor those who'd perished.

Most of the debris had been removed, and the owner who'd been out of town at the time of the explosion planned to rebuild. Bigger and even better. He would live his gayness out loud regardless of the homophobic psycho who'd blown up his own body to help "cleanse" the world. The sick man had left a suicide note in his apartment declaring that fact.

Christine and I had been able to escape, and even though our subconscious sometimes took us back to the stifling darkness and the uncertainty of life, going to therapy helped. We'd sat together twice that week, hands clasped, sharing in yet another part of moving forward.

Every day was better than the one before.

And I couldn't wait to see what all our future held.

My cell dinged, and I fished it from my pocket to find Wendy had texted me.

Doc: **Mary Rose slipped into a coma this morning.**

I'd been at her bedside the day before, checking her vitals, my heart heavy at how quickly she'd begun to fade. Much too quickly...

Eyes instantly stinging, I swallowed hard and responded that we would be there as soon as possible.

Christine hobbled out with her crutches a few minutes later, pulling me from darkness of a different sort.

I'd had many patients pass while under my care, but Mary Rose was beyond special. Her loss would affect so many people. I hoped it reminded those left behind to live life to the fullest. To accept good things when they came into their lives and hold on with all their strength because we never knew when we would breathe our last.

"What's wrong?" Christine asked the second our gazes met.

I swallowed against the thickness again—and her face fell as though reading the truth in my eyes.

"She's gone?" Christine whispered as I rose to my feet.

"Soon," I rasped.

She reached for my hand, crutch propped beneath her armpit, emerald green eyes welling with wetness. I clasped hold, squeezing, never wanting to let go.

"Forget lunch—let's go visit one last time." Her voice cracked. A tear slipped down her cheek.

Unable to say a word, I nodded.

JF

I kissed Mary Rose's warm forehead, my lips lingering as I said my goodbyes in my mind.

Heaviness.

No other word described the feeling coursing through a man while he stood beside a deathbed. Adult, child, it didn't matter.

The weight of the world, of reality, settled atop my shoulders in knowing that little Mary Rose wouldn't escape that time. She would no longer have the freedom to smile, to giggle, to laugh.

To love.

I'd been lucky as a child—and I had so many things to be thankful for. Knowing her. Making her relax when she struggled through her pain. Hearing her positivity amidst an illness that couldn't be cured for her.

Mary Rose would be missed—and I would never forget the joy she'd brought.

Stepping back, I motioned Christine forward to take the chair alongside Mary Rose's hospital bed.

So much pain had littered the happiest times of my life the previous couple of weeks. But if not having sorrow meant not having its opposite, I would embrace both with open arms.

Christine sat beside Mary Rose, holding her thin hand.

Bradley and Sophie had given us a few moments alone with their granddaughter. Still unable to speak, I simply stood behind my lover while she whispered about their good memories, fun times playing dress up, and having tea parties.

She asked Mary Rose to wear her favorite pink dress and wait for us. One day, Christine promised, she would be there too in the same bubblegum-colored outfit, and they could be fabulous together.

I fought off tears, biting my tongue. My lips. And still, Christine continued offering comfort—to both the dying girl and herself.

Christine struggled to stand, and I offered assistance so she could lean over Mary Rose to kiss her pale forehead as I had done.

"I'm going to live enough for the both of us, Rosie," Christine whispered. "I'm going to love Nurse Zimmerman as hard as I can, as long as fate allows."

A tear trickled down my cheek as Christine turned into me, burying her face against my neck. Blinking, I widened my eyes and stared at the ceiling, trying like hell not to cry.

"I love you, Jarod." The whispered words against my skin broke down the final dam inside me.

I sobbed, embracing the woman leaning against me and all aspects of life as well. Saying goodbye to my favorite little patient and finding the greatest comfort in the verbal declaration I'd been hoping to hear for entirely too long.

Chapter 30

Christine

We celebrated little Rosie with over a hundred people in attendance at a party held in her honor. Same as with the fundraiser, it was a who's who event, but no alcohol flowed, and the air held grief regardless of the video on repeat showing happier times in her life.

Jarod and I had gone together, and I got to meet his coworker, Wendy, aka Dr. Carr. Having the connection of Rosie, we greeted one another more cordially than if I'd met her the night of Rosie's ball. We both had tears in our eyes, and she offered Jarod and me best wishes in our newfound relationship.

It turned out, she'd been the one to push Jarod into trying for another go-round with me the evening of Rosie's ball. I'd turned him down, but things had turned out as they should. Had I agreed to fuck his brains out that night and shit went downhill afterward, he never would have gone to the football game with me. I might have ended up at O'Neill's with someone else—and I might not have made it out of the rubble alive.

Not one to live thinking too much about the *what-ifs*, I simply thanked the doctor, hating the crutches shoved under my armpits that made wearing heels and a fancy dress impossible while she looked sleek and sexy in her little black dress.

But Jarod didn't care what I put on or if I wore makeup. The man stayed by my side, his hand on my lower back while greeting people. He'd told me how beautiful I looked in the pink blouse I wore in Rosie's honor and the black slacks that slimmed my thighs.

And him in a black suit and tie?

He was utterly devastating to my eyes, heart, and body regardless of the somberness hovering over the hall housing our party.

Uncle Bradley, Auntie Sophie, and her sister Loretta who had arrived late, eventually ended up beside the two of us.

Uncle Bradley held out his hand to Jarod. "We can't express our appreciation enough," he said as the two men shook. "Our little Mary Rose adored you, and I know she would be excited to see you with her Chrissy. You were two of her favorite people."

Jarod's wet eyes gleamed, the corners turned down slightly, making my own throat tighten up even more. "She was an absolute doll. A breath of fresh air, and it was a pleasure to care for her. She didn't have enough time, but the joy she brought..." Jarod's voice broke, and he pursed his lips, nodding.

Her short life had held incredible value. Loving her had been worth the heartache of losing her.

I swallowed against tears, glancing over to find Dad headed toward us. Tasting a lighter dose of the grief he'd endured after losing Mom only made me love him all the more. But I wanted more for him. Hoped for it to the deepest parts of my soul.

He hugged Uncle and Auntie before turning to Loretta. A smile curved his lips, and they hugged, lingering while whispering words of condolences to one another.

Jarod lifted my hand, the brush of his lips over my knuckles turning my focus his way. Emotion poured from his eyes, and I wanted nothing more than to hold him close, press his face to my chest, and run my fingers through his hair. My heart ached for it. Add in my rubbed raw armpits from the damned crutches, and I was ready to call it a night.

We said our goodbyes which included more hugs and tears, before heading back to my house.

As he did whenever spending the night with me, Jarod helped me undress down to my panties and slid in beside me on soft sheets. But instead of shifting into his embrace, I pulled him against me and did what I'd longed to do earlier.

I held Jarod to my breast while he cried, uninhibited and vulnerable.

Had there been any question in my mind about my heart being lost to him, it rested at that moment. And once he sought out my mouth, the salt of his tears between our lips, we celebrated our own lives, further entwining our souls together.

❦

"No more crutches," I told Dad.

"Thank God," he said, his happiness clear over the cell.

"Thank fuck is more like it," I stated, firmly thrilled to have some sense of freedom back.

Being a gimp and needing help to damn near do

anything wasn't a good look on me. Bless Jarod's little heart for his persistence and his steadfastness in being beside me through it all. Surgery. PT. Bathing. Putting on my damn clothes.

The man was an absolute saint, and no one would ever be able to tell me otherwise. Sure, we got on each other's nerves, same as any other couple on the face of the planet, but the assurance of loyalty and love in actions and words offered us both a place of rest.

Home.

If given the chance to relive our time together, I would choose him all over again. From the first moment I'd set eyes on the man, I knew things would be different with him compared to my other hookups. I'd somehow recognized that my life would forever change.

And yeah...what Dad had said.

Waking from bad dreams to find Jarod cradling me in his arms, the heat of muscle and living flesh against mine, soothed me. My breaths weren't hindered, and my heart rate slowed to its usual cadence. Falling asleep once more came easier than it probably did for those without someone to hold them whenever PTSD raised its ugly head.

"I'll never be able to run a marathon," I told Dad.

He snorted with laughter. "As if you ever would anyway!"

I snickered. I wouldn't ever be a gym rat either, but I'd never been interested in fitness like Jarod was.

"I have a date Friday night."

"Huh?" I asked, sure I hadn't heard Dad right.

"I. Have. A. Date."

"Get the fuck out!" I hollered and sat up from where I'd slouched on the couch.

"What's wrong?" Jarod shouted from where he made us sandwiches in my kitchen.

"Dad's gonna get some!" I yelled back, giggling.

"Christine." I could hear the red flushing my dad's cheeks as he chided me over the phone.

"What?" I asked, still laughing. "It's about damn time."

"You wouldn't have said that a few months ago."

My jollity faded slightly. Had I not found the love of my life, I wouldn't have been as excited for Dad.

"You deserve to be spoiled again, Dad," I told him.

"It's just a date," he stated quietly.

"How long have you known her? Who is she? Anyone I've met?"

"Um..."

Another grin rocketed to my lips. "I do! Who is it, Dad? Come on...tell me! I'm dying over here!"

Jarod rounded the couch, and I glanced up, beaming at the man I loved more than anything on the planet, my dad included. He set a BLT and chips on the coffee table in front of me before joining me on the couch, his own lunch in hand.

"It's Auntie Sophie's sister. Loretta."

Loretta—I remembered how their hug had lingered and the soft smile on Dad's face as he'd held her.

"You look good together," I stated, seeing the memory clear in my mind and recognizing that fact.

"I'm hopeful, sweetheart."

My eyes welled at Dad's whisper. More than anything, I wanted him to experience the joy I did. A second chance at finding love for him but the potential to share in something just as beautiful as what he'd had with Mom.

"Me too, Dad."

Another call beeped through—Jessie. I let her go through to voicemail, continuing my chat with Dad and his plans for dinner at Loretta's. She was going to cook his favorite pot roast, and he planned to take the cabernet she loved.

Jessie rang through again, and I rolled my eyes.

"You should answer," Dad suggested, but I brushed his suggestion off, wanting to hear more about him and Loretta.

A text dinged.

Jessie: **CALL ME, YOU BITCH!**

Snorting on laughter, I bid my dad goodbye.

"Jessie actually called me a bitch," I told Jarod, still snickering while pulling up her contact info.

"What's up?" he asked around his mouthful of sandwich.

I popped a chip into my mouth, groaning over the sharp tang of vinegar along with the salt. Jarod loved every inch of my body and didn't give two shits about those freshman pounds I'd packed on in college, so I'd given up my bunny greens. Besides, the man could put together a mean-ass sandwich.

He also told me I was beautiful as-is, so I chose to believe him.

The phone rang once when I put through the call—and Jessie answered.

"I'm pregnant!"

Two surprises in a matter of minutes. My heart leapt, and I squealed for my friend. "Reid isn't gonna be a third wheel anymore!"

She laughed, and I couldn't begin to imagine her happiness—or his. Cassie would be off-the-wall silly with excitement. Jessie deserved a trophy for Mom of the Year. Unlike me, she'd been born to have babies. Selfishness dictated throughout my life that I would never attempt to procreate and be strapped down by a snotty, whining child. Such thoughts made me shudder.

Jarod proclaimed the same.

We were a match made in heaven.

Chapter 31

Jarod

Reid's son shrieked bloody murder, and I glanced up from the bundle in my arms, unsure of what to do.

"Here." Christine gestured for the tightly wrapped infant, and I gently handed the red-faced baby over. "Hey, there." Christine cooed and shushed, feathering her fingertip along the baby's light eyebrows, gently swaying from side to side.

I lowered myself onto the couch beside Reid, who beamed like a four-year-old who'd just been gifted his first baseball bat.

"Isn't he cute? He's got strong lungs. Kicks like a karate champ. Hits like one too."

I grinned, my gaze flitting back to Christine as she walked across Reid's living room to a smiling Jessie lounging in a new plush rocking chair.

"She looks good with a baby in her arms," Reid said, his voice low as Christine continued to coo to his son.

He didn't lie.

Cheeks flushed, green eyes glowing while gazing down

at that little boy...Christine stunned me near speechless. Sudden longing to see her cradling *my* child, the product of *our* love, swept over me.

"You ought to give her one."

My brow furrowed, and I half-snorted a laugh while turning back toward him. "The woman is dead set against having kids."

His dark eyes twinkled as he shrugged. "You were too once upon a time, but the way you were looking at her just now? People's desires change, Zimmerman. You of all people know this."

"I'm that obvious, huh?" I asked, once more moving my attention to Christine who handed over the baby but stayed close, smiling at the tiniest human I'd ever seen.

"He's the best thing I've ever done," Reid said, pride in his voice, "even if I haven't slept for more than two hours a night since God knows when. That boy is the sweetest gift a woman could ever give a man though. Enduring almost ten months of misery, agonizing labor..."

I glanced over at Reid to find his eyes aglow as he watched his new wife care for their son.

"I'm so fucking happy," he murmured.

I thought I couldn't be more content with what I'd been blessed with. The love of a good woman, a fulfilling day job, and friends from Elite who had remained loyal even though I'd quit. There could be more in my life, I realized at that moment, and I suddenly wanted it. But I would be fine without if the love of my life couldn't be swayed.

Christine caught my eye from the other side of the living room, swelling my heart with so much happiness I fought to breathe.

Maybe someday.

ℋ

"When are you going to give up that condo and move in here with me?" Christine asked, snuggling against my side on her couch a few hours later.

I bit back my grin and glanced down at her hand as she rubbed my thigh. It wasn't the first time she'd asked. She'd teased me forever after dropping the L word, so I'd decided to do the same whenever she begged me to combine our homes.

"I don't know. I kind of like my condo."

She pinched me and tipped back her head with a glare. "Liar. You complain about the noisy neighbors beside you every other day. Seriously though." Her gaze dropped to my lips. "You say you love me, but you're unwilling to take that step."

"I never said I was unwilling."

"Well then?"

Rather than argue, I kissed her and pulled her onto my lap, my hands skating up beneath the long Pats T-shirt she wore before bed.

No shorts. No panties.

I licked the seam of her lips and ran my thumb down over her clit.

She moaned into my mouth, opening hers to let me in for a taste. Cinnamon, sweetness, and a whole lot of sass coated her tongue. Moisture sprang to life beneath my fingers. Fuck, did I love how easily I could make her body take over her brain.

I'd long ago memorized every inch of her delightful folds, but I never tired of exploring through the slick arousal she blamed me for.

Hands on the sides of my head, she took control of our kiss, grinding her pussy against my hand.

I grabbed my waistband, shifting to free my cock from the lounge pants between me and heaven.

She pulled away, her passion-hazed eyes overcome by black pupils as she stared at me and rubbed herself against the back of my cock.

"You're so goddamn sexy," I murmured, glancing down to where she teased me.

A shift of her hips lifted her body high enough that the head of my dick brushed over her entrance.

"Promise to welcome me home like this every day?" I whispered, watching my length slowly disappear inside her wet warmth.

"God, yes," she moaned, her tight sheath swallowing me balls deep.

"Sweet girl..." We rocked together, a slow grinding dance, our gazes connected as firmly as our hearts.

"I can't get enough of you," she murmured, her tone a siren song that made my balls tingle. "Move in with me. *Please.*"

I dug my fingers into her hips and thrust upward. "I'll live with you on one condition." I decided to go for it, just to see where her mind was.

One of her auburn eyebrows arched, but she didn't stop in her maddening moves to drive my balls insane. "What's that?"

"Reconsider the whole no kids thing."

Christine stilled, searching my face.

"I know we've both been dead set against bringing children into this world, but seeing you with Reid's son..." I couldn't find the words to explain the gut-wrenching longing I'd experienced watching her hold the infant with an ease that seemed instinctive. Like she'd been born to carry our babies. Love them. Smother them with the affection she'd often spoken of how her mom had done with her.

Fear of seeing my child falling ill had always kept thoughts of having my own away, but my love for Christine and my desire to see a manifestation of how we felt for one another outweighed that slight possibility.

A soft smile curved Christine's lips. "You looked pretty damn adorable holding him too. Kinda made my ovaries explode."

Hope swelled in my chest.

"Mmm." I ran my hands up her T-shirt, palming her full breasts as she gyrated her hips again in a sensual dance that smeared her wetness over my pelvis. "So is that a maybe?" I pinched her tight nipples.

She gasped, back arching, but she didn't answer.

I rolled her nubs between two fingers, tugging with the perfect amount of pain that she shuddered, her pussy clamping around my length.

"*Definitely* a maybe," she whispered on a moan.

I thrust upward into her silken heat, working her sensitive nipples over while considering the other condition...but that one could wait. I had plans for the next few moments.

Yanking Christine forward, I captured her mouth and gave over to the need to fuck her senseless. Make her cry out my name while creaming all over my cock.

"Fuck, the things you make me desire," I groaned over her mouth, moving with abandon, desperate to fill her up with my spunk.

Soon...too soon. Didn't want it to end.

I pulled her head back so I could meet her gaze and eased into a rolling fuck, slow enough to drive us both to the brink and hold us there. She peered at me like an open book, black pupils swelled to only a ring of emerald remaining. No walls, no barricades kept me at arm's length. "Love you so much."

She whimpered and tried to move against me, but I wrapped a fist in her long tresses and wound my other arm around her waist, holding her tight.

"Give me what I want, Christine."

"Fuck me."

"I don't need to hear you begging for my dick right now." I thrust extra deep to make her moan.

She pulled at my hair, fingernails dragging over my scalp. "I love you too, now would you *kindly* fuck me so I can come already?"

Groaning, I captured her mouth again, snaking my tongue along hers as my cock took over.

Christine bounced against me, a whine building in her chest. "Oh, fuck," she ground the word out, and I thrust harder, faster into her. "Yes. Oh, God, yes!"

I buried my face in her neck and let go. My balls seized and exploded, spurting cum deep inside of her pulsing warmth aiding to milk me dry.

Sucking wind, I hugged her tight against me, filling my lungs with honeysuckle and the tangy scent of sex until both our bodies went lax.

"You moving in with me?" she asked as soon as she caught her breath.

Stubborn and driven as always. Fuck, did I love my woman.

"Sure," I tossed out, grinning like a dork.

She slapped my shoulder, and I yanked her forward to press a soft kiss to her lips, to prolong the intimacy between us. "I could get lost inside of you and still not be close enough," I murmured, once more shifting back to cradle her face in my hands. Fiery hair spilled over her shoulders, her swollen lips glistening, nose realigned to almost perfectly straight. "You're my best, the only woman I want for the rest of my life. I'll move in with you tomorrow, but right now…"

I flipped her onto her back, semi still lodged inside her lush core, and rested my forehead against hers. "Right now, I'm going to make slow, torturous love to you until you beg for release."

She tried not to smirk and failed while wrapping her legs around me. "This is feeling a lot like our first hookup."

"Mmm," I agreed, grinding my hips to coax my dick back to full thickness.

"And later?"

"Later." I pulled back and slid inside again, fighting to keep my eyes open at the slick heat of her caressing every inch of me. "Later, I'm going to ram my cock so far up your ass that you won't remember your name."

A shudder rippled down through her at my growled declaration, leaving her lips parted and pupils dilating.

I angled my hips and pressed forward against her cervix, bringing a gasp to her plump lips. *Condition two…*

"You're going to forget your name," I whispered a repeat to make sure she'd heard me, "and I'm going to call you Christine Zimmerman while filling you up with my cum. You're going to answer with a *fuck yes*."

Her lips snapped shut, eyes widening.

I leaned down and brushed my lips across hers. "Will you?"

A sparkle of mischief lit in her eyes. "*Sure.*"

Chuckling, I captured her mouth and set to work making her beg me for more.

THE END

About the Author

USA Today bestselling author Lynn Burke is a CrossFit and coffee addict. Her three spawn and two fur babies dictate how often she can be found hunched over her Mac, typing as fast as her fickle muse cooks up hot stories.

You can find more about Lynn at her website: www.authorlynnburke.com

Also By Lynn Burke

Abel's Obsession

Divulging Secrets

Healing Storms

In Between

Reluctant Lumberjack

Resisting his Mate

Billion Dollar Love Anthology

Blood Born Series

Bonds of Worship Series

Dark Leopards MC

Darkest Desires Series

Devil's Outlaws MC

Elite Escort Series

Elite Escorts MM Series

Fallen Gliders MC

Forbidden Obsession Duet

Found by Fate Series

Midnight Sun Series

Missing Link Series

Risso Family Series

Sandy Ridge Series

Sinful Nature Series

Vicious Vipers MC